I0718506

Rogues and Rebels

An Anthology

Edited by Tara Moeller

ISBN: 978-1-938215-40-7

Contents

Foreword

This is our third anthology that we've published and debuted at Marscon Williamsburg Virginia as a fundraiser for the Heritage Humane Society.

I've learned a lot about publishing anthologies, and how to get folx motivated to write and contribute. I'm still not a pro, by any means, but I'm getting better.

I've also learned a lot about pacing and not leaving things to the last minute. Projects with many contributors and a hard deadline need wiggle room. Stuff just won't happen on time, and a bunch of small setbacks can add up to being late.

That said, it's still fun reading all the great stuff that is submitted, and so far, I've been able to accept everything I get. It's all great stuff, so it isn't a bad thing.

Anyway—I hope you enjoy all these roguish, rebellious stories.

Rogues and Rebels

And don't forget to look for the little award flags for our authors. We offered a couple of challenges this year—to include "Marscon" somewhere in the story, as well as include animals. And so many of our authors did that.

And so much appreciation to John Millington and Conquest comics for the wonderful artwork for the cover! We asked and you delivered!!!

Bravo!

Until next year,

Tara

Co-Conspirators

Portfoli.Mo

Twitch.tv/TalkOfTheTavern

Rogues and Rebels

ver & Smith and the Mars Convention

By Travis I. Sivart

"I have a plan," Silver said, his brown eyes shifting to look at Hank and Diana; he swerved off the road and into the grass and sand beside it.

Silver wore his standard black gear and clothes, but with a black boonie hat over his smooth shaved scalp, and the buckles and snaps of the various belts, pouches, and straps were his signature polished silver. The cool January morning promised that it would be temperate enough that he wouldn't overheat, even in the desert-like climate.

"But is it a good plan this time?" Hank, sandwiched between Silver and Diana, held her own beige boonie hat in place with one hand, and clutched her sniper rifle with the other. "I haven't forgotten what happened when we went to Persia, and really don't want to repeat that."

"It's Iran now, as has been for centuries," Silver said, pulling the jeep out of a curve and accelerating across an open plain towards the foothills ahead, "and that wasn't my fault. There was no way I could've known they had a mystical elemental power at their beck and call. But yes, it's a good plan. Do you think these guys'll be able to keep up?"

Hank looked over her shoulder, shoving Diana to one side to see behind them. Her vest and harness jiggled and caught on the leather seat, the equipment in her satchel throwing her off balance as she turned.

"Why'd you bring all that stuff?" Silver wiped away the dust from his dark skin, slowing to enter the foothills. The vehicles behind them were closer now.

Hank turned back, rearranging the clattering gear as she did. She glared up at the dark-skinned man, her eyes narrowing.

"Look," Hank's Irish accent came in thicker as she spoke in short clipped tones, "you wear blasted black all the time, even out here. I'm wearing beige and browns, and will blend in. You carry the minimal amount, but I carry all kinds of things, because I never know what I'll need. I think it balances out, don't you?"

Silver shrugged, focusing on driving, muttering, "I missed my favorite scifi con for this? And it's their golden anniversary, too."

The open-topped jeep bounced between weed-strewn hillocks, its taupe color blending with the terrain, sand flying from under the tires. A dozen off-road vehicles followed, hot on their tail, swerving around mounds of sand and the tough grass native to the area. Armed men stood in the back of the other jeeps clutching the roll bar with one arm and an automatic rifle with the other. Drones buzzed high overhead, scouting the area and relaying the information to the rebels following Silver and Smith.

Diana leaned out the window, pushing her face forward into the wind. Hank wrapped an arm around her to keep her from flying over the short door if the vehicle hit a hummock and took an unexpected bounce. Laughing, Hank tucked her long rifle between her legs with her spare hand, before reaching up and ruffling Diana's ears.

"Does she have to do that?" Silver shouted through the thin gray scarf wrapped over his nose and mouth to keep the dust out of his lungs.

"You know she loves it," Hank grinned, hooking her hand over Diana's collar. Diana's tongue lolled as she raised her nose higher. "She's a dog, and that's what they do."

The German Shepard turned towards the two of them and wuffed, her ears forward and brow wrinkled.

"We're almost there," Silver didn't turn his head, "tell me again how Diana's going to find the Mars bracelet."

"It's a cuff and it's an artifact," Hank clarified, her voice taking on that instructor tone that it always did when she got to explain something, "not a bracelet."

"Looks like a bracelet," Silver said under his breath.

Ignoring him, Hank went on.

"We're looking for a golden cuff, about eight centimeters wide, and with a huge red coral gemstone in the center," Hank gestured, holding her fingers the approximate distance apart as she rattled off the dimensions, "it's etched with the spear and shield symbol of the god Mars, and that is bracketed by an etching of a wolf and woodpecker, both of which were sacred to Mars."

"I know all that," Silver huffed, "I know what we're looking for, I just don't understand how these rebels think some bangle will overthrow General Philonius and his despotic government."

"It's a symbol," Hank said, "and the person who has it is said to carry the blessing of Mars. That's the convention of Mars and the rule of law."

"Because the person with it is the strongest," Silver sat up straight, puffing his chest out, "and Mars was the god of war."

"Actually Mars was thought to originally have been a god of agriculture and the land," Hank gestured towards barren fields in the distance as she corrected him, "and the red coral and gold in the cuff shows the connection to the land, and protecting it and its people. But also, the men behind us probably think that this cuff has magical properties, and with it you have divine right to rule."

"If that's the case, how come they're trying to overthrow the man who has it instead of just following that divine right thing?" Silver craned his head, slowing to take a tight curve.

"Because the person with it is the strongest," Hank snickered, echoing Silver's own words back to him, "and that makes them have the divine right to rule."

Silver gave her a sidelong glare.

"And where does Diana come in for this?" he asked, accelerating, the vehicles behind him roaring around the curve to follow him in ones and twos.

"Dogs, because of their connection to wolves, are said to be able to sniff it out," Hank rumpled Diana's fur and spoke in a cutesy voice, "as if Mars himself helps them find the person and item that are best suited to rule together. Yes, he does, doesn't he?"

Diana turned and lapped at Hank's face, who squealed and pulled away, laughing.

A sandstone wall appeared in the distance, and Silver slowed and turned the jeep behind a hill. When hidden from view, he stopped the jeep, turned it off, and climbed out. The vehicles following them did the same, stopping behind other hills around them. Men leapt out as they slowed, and moved towards Silver and Hank, hunching as they ran.

The drones above split into smaller groups, some zooming higher into the morning sky, and others breaking off to circle wide around the compound.

Diana jumped down; glanced at the approaching men, and then began sniffing at the ground in a slow circle.

Hank climbed out of the vehicle, arranging her various hanging gear and bags, and pulling her weapon from the seat. As the men came closer, she spoke to them in their language, directing them to positions to keep watch. They fanned out, a small group staying behind with Hank.

Silver pulled a pair of mini-binoculars from a pouch, and crawled on his belly to the crest of the hill behind which he had parked. The sun was rising behind him, and would help hide the group's activities from the sentries. Setting the field glasses to his eyes, he surveilled the compound two kilometers in the distance.

The wall loomed ten meters over the sandy ground. Coiled reddish-brown razor wire, looped and tangled, covered the top between thick guard towers, and men with rifles paced behind the wire.

The towers rose a couple meters above the wall and tarps provided shade over the sandbag barriers of the corner structure. The tip of a machine gun peeked over edge of each makeshift nest.

Major Antonio Riva, an olive-skinned man with a thick black moustache, crawled up beside Silver and looked through his own electronic binoculars. The device hummed, recording and transmitting everything it saw to the rebel's base. There, others would dissect the information and feed positions of the enemy back to the rebels as they made their way to their target.

Riva reached over, poking Silver's arm and pointing towards the main building. Silver looked through his binoculars again, focusing on where the Major had indicated.

The structure was set up in a square, with a large courtyard in the middle filled with a garden of flowering trees and plants, a fountain in the center. Raising his binoculars higher, Silver focused on the communications array on top of the command building. An a-frame structure of metal pylons supported various receiving and broadcasting dishes and devices.

After a few minutes, the two men exchanged looks, and nodded to one another. They slid backwards until they would not be seen by the enemy guards, stood, and returned to the others.

"Okay," Silver checked his weapons and pouches, making sure everything was in place, "our intel was good. The plan stands. Hank, you need to get in close enough to hack their wireless system and take down the electronic defenses. Riva, once Hank signals the all-clear, you take your team and hit them with the main attack on one side, and I'll slip in the secondary door with Diana on the other side. Once in, Diana and I will search out the artifact inside the building and notify you once I have it. With their forces divided and in confusion, and their security systems down, a third assault team will then hit the main gate, which is where we'll gather to make our exit."

Looking around, Silver watched the heads of the men and women gathered nodding, their expressions grim. This was the final fight that would determine if they freed their country from a corrupt dictator, or if the last vestiges of rebellion were wiped away.

"Everyone's comms up?" Silver tapped his own earpiece and body cam then gave a thumbs up.

Once everyone had mirrored his actions, they turned and headed towards the compound.

The ground shook as the wall on the other side of the sandstone compound exploded. Voices shouted and the dunes and grass absorbed the sound of the sharp bark of weapon fire.

The five rebels accompanying Silver were a few meters away, facing outward, hidden and watching for any movement.

Silver waited, Diana at his feet. The German Shepard's ears swiveled constantly, following sounds as they happened, and her nose scented the air, then the ground around Silver, then the air again.

Silver checked his gear again; making sure everything was in place. He left his gun strapped into the holster, and pulled out an expandable electro-shock baton.

Diana looked at the baton, then up at Silver's face, her head cocked and wrinkles appearing on her forehead.

"Less noise," Silver explained to the dog in a whisper, "just a crackle and a soft pop, but the gun makes a lot more noise and draws lots more attention. And that means more men, more guns, and more chances of dying. We want to avoid that, right?"

Diana wuffed softly, watching Silver.

"Glad we agree on that." Silver checked the counter on his cardphone, which was attached to the bracer on his wrist. "Okay, it's about time to go. Look at me, talking to you like you understand every word. Ain't that the silliest thing?"

Diana let out a sigh with a huff and turned away to look at the door set into a shadowed alcove of the wall.

"We just need to wait for the all-clear from Hank," Silver squatted on his haunches, stroking Diana's neck, "but don't worry, the Hawk has never let me down. She'll get it."

Hank lay atop a grassy knoll, her partial ghillie suit – more a cloak of grass-like material with a small, tented hood that covered her head and arms when they were extended – concealing her from the guards on the wall. She had to get to the highest point she could to catch the strongest signal of the compound to hack it.

A small team of two women and a man hid in the brush around the hill Hank was on, ready to distract any patrols or defend Hank. They all hunkered down and the wall exploded, just a couple dozen meters away, shattering under the onslaught of the rebels tasked with the distraction tactic. It had to seem like a real enough threat to pull all attention away from every other morning task. Hank was confident that the shift change, due to be taking place right now, was in chaos.

Hidden under the cover of her grass cloak, Hank unrolled her graphene keyboard and monitor. With a few keystrokes on the paper-thin material, the keyboard lit up and showed the light-outlined keys, and then she linked the two devices and began working her magic.

Minutes passed as she traced signals, narrowed down passkeys, and used complex algorithms to crack into the cyber-shell of the network that stood like a beacon in the middle of the grasslands. She smiled and giggled, and with a flourish pressed the final keystroke to bring down all the defenses. A hum, unnoticed before, disappeared from the audible range of human hearing as the electronic cordons in the doors, windows, and gates of the complex went dead. The electric buzz that ran through the thick, braided wires, and the thin crisscrossed chain-link sheets, that covered the surface of the outer wall went silent.

Pressing a button on her wrist bracer, Hank activated the rebel's private channel, saying, "Defenses are down, it's a go. I repeat, all defenses are down, go, go, go!"

As she shouted that into her comm, she heard the sound of a drone buzzing past overhead and the rapid-fire bark of automatic weapons as the rebels guarding her shot at the intruding enemy craft.

The door swung loose, its magnetic lock disengaged when Hank took out the defenses. Moving into the building, Silver cleared the corners on each side of the interior of the door and waved the first three rebels past him to run to the hall intersection ahead.

Diana stayed by Silver's side, sniffing at the ground and air in turn, and watching the men as they moved from one position to the next. Leap-frogging past one another, the group made its way deeper into the complex. They turned the fifth corner, and the chatter of weapon fire filled the air from the right.

The rebels dropped prone or to their knees, leaning around the corner and firing at the enemy from the safety of cover, more shouts came from behind. They'd been flanked.

With a series of barks, Diana took off down the hall to the left.

Silver's head swiveled back and forth, from the men engaged in a firefight, to Diana who was fast disappearing into the distance. That dog was the only one who would be able to track down the artifact.

Heaving a sigh, Silver turned to follow the German Shepard, zigging and zagging down the hall to avoid the enemy gunfire that popped behind him, striking the walls and floor around him as he ran.

Turning a corner, Silver saw Diana disappearing around the next corner, far in the distance. He ran after her, pushing himself to move fast enough to keep up, but slow enough that he didn't run into trouble without being aware. Careening around another corner, bouncing off the wall, he spun into the center of a four-way intersection. Diana was nowhere in sight.

To his right was an open passage that showed daylight and the green growth of the courtyard, straight ahead was a long hall that led past dozens of doors, and to his left was a short hall that ended in a flight of stairs that led down.

Separated from the group, and having no idea where Diana was, except for distant echoing barks, Silver hesitated, trying to decide which way to go.

The wall above his head burst into a cloud of dust, bullets ripping through the plaster and mortar. Ducking, Silver ran down the hall to his left without a second thought.

Hank's three guards scattered, running for better cover than the valley between hills allowed them. Three drones zoomed in, firing darts with an audible puff of air, which whistled a high-pitched whine as they shot towards their targets. One rebel, the man, went down clutching at his buttocks where a dart had sprouted. One of the women let out a small shriek, and Hank saw the rebel's hand fly to the side of her neck to pluck a dart from it. The woman's eyes rolled into the back of her head and her body folded in upon itself; she went face down into the dirt, unconscious.

The remaining woman, butt of her rifle planted firmly against her shoulder and head held slightly tilted to look down the sight of the weapon, fired, moving backwards. One drone exploded. A second shot, and another drone spun out of control and vanished from sight. The third drone whipped towards the woman, and the rebel took off running, disappearing around the hill.

The drones should have been disabled, Hank thought, *I shut down everything that was attached to the defense systems. Unless the drones are recent addition to their tech, then they'd be on their own circuit. They were probably even sub-contracted from an independent firm, and because of that weren't linked to the same server as everything else!*

"You!" A heavily accented baritone voice called out in English, "You, under the grass blanket, come out! Move slow and keep your hands where we can see them!"

"Captain Murdock," a younger man's voice called, speaking in the local language, "the other rebel is getting away. Should we go after her?"

"No," Murdock growled, answering in the same language, "the hunter drones can take her out, we have our prey here."

Moving as little as possible, Hank folded her computer and tucked it into her satchel with one hand, sliding the other hand down the barrel of her rifle.

Silver ran down the stairs onto the landing, rebounded off the wall, and stumbled around the corner and down the second half of the flight. Tripping into another intersection at the bottom, shouts coming from above and behind, he paused to get his bearings.

It was cooler down here, and no windows let in natural light. He was underground. Diana's barking had gotten louder and closer. The hall to the left opened into what looked like a large chapel, to the right was a hall with more doors on each side and one at the end.

Straight ahead was a set of double doors, the thin window in each showing some sort of cafeteria beyond. Dozens of soldiers sat at long tables, eating plates of scrambled eggs, sausages, and various other foods. Televisions, mounted in the corners of the room, blared out the gunshots of a classic action movie and the men stared at the screen or chatted with one another.

Silver dodged to his left, crouching and pressing against the wall closest to the stairs.

The sound of two sets of booted feet, approaching fast, came from up the stairs. If the men on the stairs were noticed by the men in the cafeteria, everything they had done to get this far could come to a quick end. Silver readied his batons and waited, his eyes shifting from the oblivious men at the tables, to the stairs.

The sound of Diana's barking quieted and then died out.

The two soldiers came barreling down the stairs into the hallway. Silver's hands shot forward, batons out. With a muffled pop and crackle, electric charges went off - one into the belly of one of the men, and the other in the neck of the other man — and with a gurgled cry of surprise, the men collapsed, twitching.

A soldier at the table closest to the doors, looked over, his brow furrowed. He craned his head, looking for the source of the odd noise outside the door. Not seeing anything, he stood and went towards the doors to investigate.

Silver pulled the two men by their ankles towards the chapel, the assault rifles dragging behind them by the straps that were around the men's bodies. As he hauled the men out of sight, one of the men's guns caught on the corner of the doorway leading into the room. Silver heard the TV volume grow louder as the cafeteria door opened.

Yanking on the man's foot, trying to pull the weapon free of the corner, the gun clattered against the floor. Dropping to his belly, Silver fell between the two men and pressed down on the gun, silencing it. His head was just past the doorway, giving him a view of the soldier from the lunchroom. The uniformed man was looking to his left, away from Silver. The sound of the TV from the rec room filled hall, "You've got to ask yourself one question: 'Do I feel lucky?' Well, do ya, punk?"

came the sound of the movie from beyond
the soldier.

Silver grabbed the gun, lifted it, and
pulled it around the corner, ducking his
head back just as the man turned to look
towards him. The sound of the TV quieted
and clunk of the rec-room door closing
echoed in the hall. The thump of boots on
the stone floor approached where Silver
hid.

Silver looked for his batons. They were
on the floor near his, and the unconscious
soldiers', feet. He grabbed the rifle,
flicking the safety off and holding it
ready for the other man's head to appear
around the doorway. The gunfight in the
movie had kept the mess hall full of
soldiers unaware of the previous attack,
but Silver knew that any more shots would
alert the whole cafeteria of the
situation.

The sound of the movie rose again as
the door behind the approaching soldier
opened. A voice, not in English, called
out something and the approaching soldier

laughed and responded, his voice shrinking further away as he did. The two voices faded and the mess hall door closed behind them.

Silver let out a breath he hadn't realized he was holding and rolled over.

Sitting up, he looked around the chapel. In the front of the room, at the foot of the dais, sat Diana with her head cocked to one side.

Beside her was a pedestal covered with red velvet. Atop the cushioned platform was a golden cuff, polished to a high shine. In the center of the jewelry was a deep red circle of coral.

Hank twisted, rolling from her belly to her back, the ghillie suit flying away from her as she brought her weapon to bear and fired it. The Captain dove to the side, rolled, and came up on his feet, the dirt where he had been standing exploding in a puff of sand.

Hank jerked her rifle towards the man, but he disappeared around the side of the hill. Shots erupted around her, sand flying into the air, and she threw herself down the far side of the mound. Rolling as she did, tucking Sydney—the name she had given her custom-built rifle—against her midsection, she came up running at the bottom, dodging around the terrain.

The patrol pursued her. Captain Murdock screamed orders, demanding she be captured or killed.

Hank mashed her cardphone to activate the comm channel to the rebels. It blinked red, showing that it couldn't connect. *Jammed*, she thought. That meant the base wasn't getting any information, either. How could that be?

Sprinting around another hill, Hank drew up short. Five enemy soldiers knelt in front of her, their weapons leveled directly at her.

Silver burst into the courtyard, the Mars cuff tucked into one of his many pouches, the main gate just across the gardens. Pressing the notification key on his cardphone on his bracer, to let everyone know to converge on the front entrance and get out of here, it flashed red. He pressed it again. The phone blazed the same warning, 'No network or connection' in a bright red pulsating glow.

A crackle of energy and a crack of sound came from behind Silver. He felt something coil around his throat, and he came up short, pulled from his feet. He fell hard on his knees, grabbing at his throat; a metal flex-coil crackled with energy under his grip.

Silver's hands vibrated as he clutched the constricting cable, and electricity burst through it. The black man's vision swam and he listed to the side, his throat closing, and his oxygen supply closing off. The world burst into white, then a spectrum of color, and then everything went dark.

Falling to the ground, his hands shooting out to his sides in a stiff forced rictus, he heard Diana growl, then bark, and then the scramble of her claws on cobblestones as she ran, leaving him to his fate.

Good, he thought, darkness overtaking him, *as least one of us might get out of this alive.*

Hank faced the makeshift firing squad. Murdock's shrill command came from the hilltop she had just abandoned.

"Kill her!" the Captain screeched in English.

Hank smirked and shook her head. Dropping her weapon and raising her hands above her, she looked up to the heavens.

"Why," she said in the language of the soldiers in front of her, "does everyone underestimate me?"

Crossing her wrists above her head, she looked directly at the enemy with a crooked smile. When her two wrist bracers made a connection, they interfaced with the targeting software in her contacts and zeroed in on the soldiers watching her with a confused look. Buttons from her vest activated, firing forward towards the troops with blinding speed, and exploding as they connected with the men.

Gunfire barked as the fingers of the soldiers reacted to the impact, bullets flying through the air. Most missed Hank, she stood plainly in their sights, but one took her in the shoulder, and another hit her in the left thigh. She spun like a ragdoll, flying backwards.

The sand exploded in front of her, and the five men flew in all directions, screams cut off as the explosives – or the sudden landing on rock and dirt – did the final blow to them.

Captain Murdock stared, his eyes wide and his mouth open. His men lay unmoving at the foot of the hill. Movement, from the woman he had ordered killed, drew his attention.

"You suck," Hank spat, rolling to a sitting position, and snatched up Sydney and fired one shot.

The man's head snapped back, and then lolled forward, his gaze connected with hers for a few seconds before his eyes went blank and he fell backwards, unmoving.

Hank heard a cheer from the courtyard on the other side of the wall, and then the voice of the man who they had come to overthrow spoke over a loudspeaker or a bullhorn of some sort.

"Hang him," General Philonius shouted in his native tongue, "hang him, until he is dead!"

Hank lurched forward, her shoulder and thigh throbbing. Her graphene armor had absorbed both shots - though there was a hole in it where each projectile had hit — but that didn't stop the bone-deep bruising that she would have to deal with right now and in the upcoming weeks.

The 'Hawk' looked for a way to fix this problem, her mind and eyes searching a thousand possibilities and options. She needed a vantage point, someplace high, where she could see everything, and where Sydney had an opportunity for a shot.

The compound was cleared of trees, so no chance of using one to get a clear view of the situation. It looked like the only way to get what she needed was to get on the wall.

Subdued fighting still came from the first insertion point as the rebels continued their distraction, but it was significantly less than what it has been even just a few minutes ago, the sound of weapons' fire infrequent and stuttered. They may have been overwhelmed.

Hank limp-ran towards the wall, seeing the guards facing inward to watch whatever spectacle was taking place inside the courtyard. Slinging Sydney over her shoulder, she threw herself up the sandstone barricade, catching the chain link fencing embedded in the wall.

Her shoulder screamed in protest and she hissed a breath of pain. Pausing for the briefest moment - where she really wanted to give up, drop to the ground, and crawl away – she pulled herself together, and forced herself to lift her leg up and shove the toe of her booted foot into the diamond-shaped opening of the defunct electrified fencing cemented into the wall. It was her left leg, and lightning shot - from where the bullet had torn through her armor - to her hip, and her footing slipped.

Panting and hanging from her fingers, Hank pulled herself together and slowly repeated the action. Meter by agonizing meter, she forced herself up the wall of the tower. Long minutes passed as she fought for every centimeter, every arm-length, and every time she pulled herself up it was another small victory.

Finally, she pulled herself up and looked over the edge of the sandbags. The guard's back was to her, his gun hanging at his side, and the machine gun nest abandoned.

Hanks's mind went through dozens of ways to dispatch the man. Push him over the edge, but then the crowd in the courtyard would see it. Throwing him over the outside wall risked him surviving and raising the alarm. Shoot him and they would hear, even with the sound-dampening device on her weapon. Choke him out, and there was a good chance that he would overpower her with his greater weight and strength. A knife into vital parts was never as quick as it was in the movies. Then it came to her, the best way to do this unnoticed.

Hank pulled herself over the wall of sandbags, holding back any grunts of pain, and moving with as much stealth as her body would allow. She kept one hand on her various jingling bits and bobs to make sure the guard wasn't clued in to her approach - though the shouts and cheers from the courtyard could probably cover the clumsy approach of Dumbo the elephant and all seven dwarves — and with her other hand drew a small device from a pocket in her satchel.

Her ankle twisted, and she let out a small squeak as her thigh surged with pain. The man spun, a confused look on his face turning to alarmed surprise. Hanks's hand shot out, and she slapped the stamp-sized device with eight small needles on the back into the side of his neck.

The device was meant for plugging into a computer, disrupting the flow of electric and information to a machine. She had meant to press it into the back of his neck, into the spine, hoping it would have a similar effect, discharging its stored static charge to stun him into unconsciousness.

The man went stiff, but a high-pitched squeal came from his mouth.

Hank grabbed his neck with her other hand, her own eyes wide, and pulled his face into her bosom, smothering the noise as the crowd roared again at the spectacle below.

The man shook and quaked, then went still and slid down Hank's body to the ground.

Panting, her heart pounding, Hank's mind expected gunfire and blossoming pain any second. It didn't come.

Creeping to the edge of the machine gun nest, she peeked at the scene below.

The men and women of General Philonious's army stood in a semi-circle around a gallows, a wooden platform with a hangman's noose dangling from an overhead beam, cheering. Silver wobbled between two guards, each holding one of his arms, a third man sliding a rope around Hank's partner's neck.

The General, an older man with salt and pepper hair, a thick moustache, and dozens of medals on his breast, stood on one side of the platform with his hands on his hips and a victorious smile on his face.

"This," General Philonius gestured at Silver, speaking in the local language, "is what happens to rebels and enemies of the state. They die!"

Hank's thoughts jumbled as she knelt, bringing Sydney up and going through what needed done. She had to take out the jamming device, and she had to save Silver. But which one first?

She wanted to shoot the General. She wanted to take out the men holding her partner during his final moments. But the priority had to be freeing an imprisoned country.

Pressing her eye to the scope, she panned Sydney upward, scanning the communications tower atop the compound's main building. There. Near the top of the metal-pylon array was new dishes, showing what would be the devices she hadn't disabled before. The jamming technology.

If she could just—she closed her mind to distraction—find the power lead to this array, the power that fed the jamming devices, then she could alert the rebels to come in full force, and attack the dictator while he was distracted.

Slowing her breathing, she found the junction box, and let her scope move in a slow figure eight around her target.

The crowd cheered again, and Hank opened her other eye to see Silver with a noose around his throat and the General standing next to the lever that would drop the trapdoor from under Silver's feet.

She couldn't let that distract her.

Closing her one eye again, she focused on her shot, counting her breaths, waiting for the rhythm to tell her when to take the shot.

The General shouted something, and the sound of the hatch dropping synchronized with the gentle caress of Hank's finger on her trigger. Sydney jumped in her hands, and the pop of the junction box exploding was lost the roar of the gathered people below.

Hanks looked to her cardphone. The red warning of 'no network' was gone.

She mashed the notification button, and the message went out to every rebel in range to move in and attack.

The roar of the spectators was overwhelmed by the sound of renewed gunfire from outside the walls. Dozens of drones rose over the barricade and dropped from high altitudes as the rebels set the final stage of the attack into motion.

Pressing her eye back to the scope, Hank swung Sydney from the tower to her partner.

Silver hung by his neck, his hands secured behind his back, and his legs jerking, struggling for air in the noose, a half dozen feet above the ground.

Rebels burst into the compound, enemy guards falling under the onslaught.

General Philonius screamed in rage, drawing out a sidearm and aiming it at Silver.

Hank had to choose; shoot the rope or shoot the dictator. If she chose the rope, Silver would be able to breath, but the General might kill him before he could recover. If she shot the dictator, then Silver might die before she could get the rope, which was a million to one shot anyway.

Hank's scope went from one target to the other, her mind frozen with indecision.

A low and fast black and beige form darted forward across the gallows.

Diana.

The German Shepard launched herself through the air, her teeth latching onto the General's forearm, and throwing his aim off target. The shot went wide.

Hank whipped her barrel back to the rope above Silver's head. Slowing her breathing again, she waited for the shot.

Something hit her from behind. Her head jerked to the right, and the shot went wide. She fell to her side, the pain in her shoulder blossoming as she hit the ground.

The guard she had thought she had taken out stood above her. He held a rifle pointed at her, a cruel smile on his face.

Ignoring the pain, Hank spun her legs around, catching the man's legs and knocking him prone.

Pushing to her feet, she turned to look at Silver. His breath was ragged, his eyes bulging, and his movements slowing.

The guard behind her rose to his feet, bringing his gun to bear.

Hank looked at him over her shoulder, smiled, then turned towards Silver, firing Sydney from her hip, once, then twice, then a third time.

The rope around Silver's neck split, but didn't break from the first shot, causing him to swing back and forth and spin in a slow circle. The second shot missed completely. But the third shot cut the rope, and Silver fell to the ground.

The guard fired, point blank, into Hank's back.

Silver gasped a ragged breath of air, rolling onto his back and pulling his bound arms under his butt and legs. Reaching up, he loosened the rope from his neck, his vision spinning.

He shook his head to clear his sight, but it only made the world spin more.

He stopped, squinted, and slowly looked around. He focused on a single gunshot, his hearing drawing his eyes to a guard tower above him. Hank lay slumped over the sandbags of the machine gun nest, an angry soldier looming over her and taking careful aim with his rifle at her head.

Silver rolled to one side, grabbing the sidearm of a fallen guard, and dropping to his back. He jerked the gun upward, firing, pulling the trigger repeatedly. Sandbags exploded as the line of bullets worked their way upward. The guard looked down at Silver, surprised, as the final bullet caught the man and threw him backwards.

Silver watched Hank roll over, the pain in her movements obvious, and fire Sydney at the now unseen target, again and again.

Silver stumbled to his feet and out from under the gallows. Looking back and atop it, he saw Diana ravaging General Philonious's arm, the mad dictator bringing his pistol to bear on the dog.

Silver didn't hesitate; he jerked the weapon up and pulled the trigger. It clicked, but didn't fire.

The General lowered his gun to Diana's head.

Silver threw the useless weapon in his hand at the dictator. It flew through the air, hitting the man in the temple.

Philonius's head ratcheted to one side, and he fell, his gun flying from his hand. Diana released her grip on his arm, and launched herself at his throat.

Hank grunted as the medic wrapped her midsection. Her thigh was already bound, and her arm was in a sling. Sydney hung over her other shoulder.

Silver leaned back against their jeep, running his finger along the ligature marks on his neck, Diana at his feet, happily gnawing on the beef jerky that he tossed down to her.

"It'll give her gas," Hank remarked.

"It's ok," Silver smiled, "she's willing to pay the price, and deserves a reward."

"So, that was your plan?" Hank's tone was snide. "Go in, stir up a hornet's nest, and get hung?"

"Hey," Silver never looked up from tossing jerky to Diana, "I've always been hung, but it's nice to have others see it once in a while."

Hank rolled her eyes.

"Besides," Silver continued, "this one wasn't my fault. You're the one who missed the second set of communication arrays."

"Ugh," Hank pushed the medic away, "can we just go home now? We have an antique store that needs our attention."

Follow the continuing adventures of Silver and Smith in Travis I Sivart's books.

Blaved: Only the Good Parts – Part 1

By Andrew Hiller

The wine Margarine Snifter sipped drew a rosy blush to her cheeks despite its bitter crabapple aftertaste. She arched her eyebrows, noting the untouched glasses around her. The sniggering faces. Something scratched and burned along her throat. Her fingers tightened along the stem of the fluted glass. She raised a heavy palm to her cherry lips to catch a cough, hoping not to spot blood. Margarine was pretty certain that the prince had just poisoned her. She had no understanding of why. Perhaps it had to do with the loss of the three ships.

Dabbing at her lips with a napkin monogramed with her fiance's initials, her eyes drew closed. She felt gladdened that her last experience, had at the very least, included a good vintage. And so, with an exaggerated sigh, one that might draw gasps from theatre goers watching a melodrama, Margarine swooned, lolling back in her chair, releasing behind her a cascade of almond hair that broke loose in an amber waterfall.

The Prince turned to his henchman with an exaggerated sigh, staring sadly at the spill of red soaking into the tablecloth.

"Shame to waste such a good bottle of the '49."

"It is certain to stain," the henchman nodded, leaving the prince to swirl his own unsampled wine.

"Stemish wine knows no equal," he said in a voice filled with despair.

We're going to skip ahead. For the next thirty pages the author, Goldman, expounds on the excellent quality of Stemish wines and how unequaled it is in all respects. In this effort, he degrades its French, Spanish, and Italian counterparts, saying that they all fail in terms of color, bouquet, and richness. More, Goldman reminds us that the perfect Stemish climate and rich soil has made it the envy of the grape world since Charlemagne, but as we are sure the reader already knows this and likely has a bottle stashed away for important occasions; it is unnecessary to include all thirty pages here.

Drugged and unconscious, Margarine's fiancé, Prince Lumpadunk and his henchman, a chess grandmaster from East Athens, New Amsterdam, dragged poor Margarine towards an ermine balcony overlooking a crescent moon where they had preset a window washer's platform.

But just before tossing her onto the awaiting swing stage, the Prince paused.

"She really is quite lovely," Lumpadunk declared with a twist of sour lips.

In fact, Margarine Snifter had been pronounced the sixth most beautiful woman in the world by her fifteenth birthday. Although her standing had recently fallen from her previous high (fourth) for declaring, against all possible reason, that astronomical data proved that the

Rogues and Rebels

Earth was round. This pronouncement, as you can well imagine, was not taken well at all by those who rate loveliness. After all, internal beauty counts heavily in the final tally and several judges raised the point that anyone who fell for the balderdash of the Round-Earthers could not be truly beautiful (This downgrading was somewhat tempered by Margarine's role in developing three vaccines.)

Again, we will skip ahead because who really wants to read a 500-page macroeconomic discussion of peasant pharmacology? Furthermore, dear readers, if you read your Billingsly [and you must read your Billingsly if you wish to get anywhere in life] you will have a keen idea of where the author stands.

The pair loaded Margarine Snifter onto a swinging platform supported by four ropes held still by a winch. A trio of rapscallions, a French longbowman, a dwarf, and Greek strategist, awaited with a cart below to spirit her away. Lumpydrink cranked once before pausing.

"When I came up with the plan to trade her for a barrel of Dutch tulips I thought it quite brilliant."

"It was, sire," the Grandmaster toadied.

"But now, I'm wondering if I have misjudged the price of commodities." The Prince scratched an overlong jaw chiseled with a cavernous dimple, "If tulips are prized not for their rarity, but brevity of beauty than what of woman?"

"A woman of such genius as Margarine Snifter will remain beautiful because of her contributions and humors for a long time." The Grandmaster considered, "It stands to reason then, that in terms of scarcity, our dear Margarine is far less valuable than a flower."

Lumpadunk nodded and the pair recommenced the work of lowering her. A third of the way down, the Prince stopped again. He watched his soon to be ex-fiancé swaying slightly on her platform. His heart throbbed like an unpopped kernel of corn that yearned to explode just once.

Margarine had such perfect kneecaps, he thought. *No wonder everyone falls fell for her. Why even the bricks of the castle wall blush at her touch.*

"And yet," the Prince said, pulling back on the brake again, "She will be missed. What if the peasants revolt?"

"The peasants are always revolting."

A rimshot sounded off in the distance. And the pair began to lower her again, but just as Margarine neared the ground, the grandmaster jerked his head.

"What was that?"

"It must have been thunder."

"Thunder on a clear night with nary a cloud in the sky? Inconceivable."

"Beware plagiarism, my lord."

From a distance, the rumble grew closer as the man in corduroy approached.

"The Dire Brigand Bob?"

The chess grandmaster had sent him on a wild goose chase through the Valley of Sanity, the Liquid Desert, and the Steppe Aerobic. This, he calculated, should have him distracted for months, but the glint of his steed's teeth filled with fine Stemish silver fillings left little doubt... Margarine's true friend had found their trail once again.

"Incon—"

The Grandmaster cut him off with a nasty look.

"Well, it is."

"I think we have been checked. It seems the Man in Corduroy will his collect his debt."

"Damn! I knew I shouldn't have bet Margarine in that foul poker game, but I had such a hand! Two pair!"

"I warned you not to blave."

The pair looked at the charging figure. Below the rapscallions hurried onto their cart to drive off, afraid of the Man in Curduroy's famed prowess. Once, in a single day, he had outrank a dwarf proving his endurance, outshot a British longbowman providing evidence of his skill, and outtalked an auctuioneer demonstrating the nimblest of tongues. The

Man in Curduroy was a man to be reckoned with.

Lumpadunk and the Grandmaster considered. Margarine hung suspended barely two Fezzik's from the ground.

With every moment, the man in corduroy loomed closer.

"Do you suppose we could buy him off?"

The chess grandmaster ran variations through his head. Slowly, he raised his finger.

"It's possible. Do you have a mutton lettuce and tomato sandwich?" he asked, "I hear they're very good."

Captain of the Seas

By Emberly Summers

Racing along the sandy shoreline.
Coarse golden flecks of dust
caress my ivory skin.
The salty air tingles
on my parched lips
the scorching sun
dampens my aching bones in sweat.

Pushing forward,
ignoring my exhaustion
drawn to the emerald depths.
Like a siren's lament
cast to lost explorers
buried out at sea.

A lustful gleam fills my eyes.
Proudly boarding the grand vessel,
with weathered planks of wood
marking the passage of time.

Rogues and Rebels

Drifting across the open waters.
gliding effortlessly on marbled ice
while staring out into the blazing
horizon,
Inhaling the zesty air billowing behind my
vessel
guiding the white clouds sails made of
parchment.

Fueled by the rush of the hunt
for gems that sparkle in the golden sun.
Beckoned by the lure of adventure.
Never belonging to any other mistress but
the sea.

Silent predator

By Emberly Summers

Blanketed by ink black darkness of night
Specks of moonlight illuminate the ominous
abyss
The witching hour looming in the distance
Slithering through
the slumbering city streets

Chasing after my prey
In hopes of ensnaring my prize
Desperate to extract safe guarded secrets
entombed in the depths of their mind.
Afraid of their impending fate
Of crossing the silent predator.

As the bell tolls the victims final hours
It's failed attempts to outsmart me
trying to use my pride as an allusive
distraction
Only to fall heedlessly into my hidden
trap

Rogues and Rebels

sealing their misfortunate before their
soul
is claimed by my gleaming sword

Sterling Fox

By Jeffrey S. McGuire

The rook called out from the trees above. Fox vaulted over the hollowed log in the path, landing on all fours in the wet earth on the other side. She wiped her dirty hands on the thighs of her pants, twisting the fabric between her fingers as she scanned the treetops. The same bird had followed the party for three days. Fox couldn't see any black feathers amongst the glitter of sun filtering through the leaves. Her red curls bounced around her shoulders and her face colored from exertion as she darted after the party's guide, Jori, who'd gotten too far ahead for her liking.

She had been trying to keep no more than twenty paces between herself and Jori, but the gangly man with the toothy grin moved quick as hare through the underbrush. It would be easier to keep up if Fox were in her animal form, but no one else in the party knew she possessed such magic. A thief's best skill was keeping secrets.

A swift glance over Fox's shoulder brought cool relief against the hot dread pooling in the pit of her stomach. Hawthorne, and his master, Alavanja, had made it over the log. The fourth and most pungent member of their troupe, Erskine, a barbarian of a man, thick and sinewed, dumber than a sack of rocks, landed more gracefully in the mud than she had managed to.

"Not too much further." Jori's accent twisted around his words tighter than the bramble thicket they'd encountered yesterday.

Fox measured the guide's words with a grain of salt. Jori lead the group away from the game trail on their second morning and then taken them on a Southwestern course. Today he changed directions again, heading mostly to the

East. Something smelled off, and it wasn't the barbarian.

The previous night's storm remained trapped beneath the canopy, the humid air thick in the back of Fox's throat, like trying to breath underwater. Jori eased North and the party followed like ducklings behind their mother. Fox ground her teeth together in irritation and promised herself that the first thing she'd do when this adventure ended would be punch the collector, Nicklaus. Joining this quest, following this lost guide had been his doing. The quest was too much for the idol of a dead god. If the collector were here, he'd tell Fox she was wrong, that someone somewhere would pay handsomely for their own slice of history.

Nicklaus wasn't here, though. He was safely back on East street in the capitol, tending to the air ships that brought precious cargo, trading in rare artifacts and treasures he *procured*. A hefty percentage of the items in *Nicklaus' Antiquities & Collectibles* were brought to him by his agents, more commonly known as thieves. Fox was the best. She thought her reputation would have at least earned her a reprieve from adventuring, but such as it was, the reward for good work was always *more work.*

Alavanja, the benefactor of this journey into the wilds, could have easily been Fox's great-grandfather. It was a wonderment that the spindly aged dodderer was able to keep pace with the rest of them. Fox suspected that he too possessed some kind of magic, figuring he stored in the scraggly white beard that hung to his navel, an homage to every hair that had vacated his shiny bald head.

The old man and his assistant, Hawthorne, burst into *Nicklaus' Antiquities & Collectibles* after the last snowfall of the winter, when it was too warm for the flakes to stick to the roads, but still too cold for rain. The bird, Tevan's, pebbly squawk and ruffled feathers when the shop's bell rang caught Fox's attention and Hawthorne held it. She abandoned the puzzle box she'd been fiddling with in favor of watching the cloaked men stamp slush from their boots. The younger of them, his name Hawthorne, though she hadn't known it in that moment, pushed the white fur-trimmed hood back from his face, cocked his head, and smiled crookedly at her. A gnarled pink scar ran from the left corner of his mouth across his cheek and ended almost at his temple like someone had tried to draw a crescent moon on his face with a dull knife. The mark didn't detract from the pleasantness of his other features, storm gray eyes, aquiline nose, full lips, and square jaw with at least two days' worth of dark beard.

"Hello?" He called out. His smooth baritone made Fox's heart drop into her stomach and then leap into her throat. Nicklaus came out of his office to greet them. The collector patted Fox's small furry head and scratched behind her ear as he made arrangements to find some treasure that the old man called the **Marscon**. Fox wished she were back in the shop, now. The must of old leather-bound books far more appealing than the scent of Erskine. Even down wind, bringing up the rear, Fox still had to wipe away the tears brought to her eyes by the old cheese aroma.

Fox needed a vacation. Maybe when she got out of this forest she'd take Tevan to the coast. They could sit on the sandy shore, human with no Nicklaus or animal forms, and suck down as many tankards of fruity ale as their livers would reasonably allow.

Jori stopped and waited for the rest of the group to catch up. "We are here." He reached up and yanked a handful of ivy from what Fox assumed was a tree. The vine tore away with the sound of ripping fabric as the shallow roots lost their hold on the stone. Fox stared up at the column, admiring the perfectly aligned and stacked rock towering two men tall. A few paces away stood another column, then another, set out like footprints on a map.

"It's just as I thought it would be," said Alavanja gazing, misty-eyed, at the path. Giddiness perforated the weak rasp of his voice. He clapped his hands together and for a brief moment seemed to forget his age, striding forward with a speed that required Fox to take two steps for every one of the old man's.

Stone pavement stretched between the columns and the further they walked the less ruined the structures became until gradually they began passing beneath great stone arches. The wilderness enhanced the unmapped ruins, almost as though the builders had intended them to become indistinguishable from the forest itself. Honeysuckle hung in clumps and wreaths of red and yellow. Bees flitted amongst the vine's delicate white blossoms. Fox shooed one of the insects from her face with a gentle brush of her hand.

"Hate stinging things," said Erskine swatting at the bees, his meaty arms thrashing through the air like the broken propeller of an airship.

"If you leave them be, they won't bother you." Fox called over her shoulder.

The graveled caw of the rook sounded once more, the harsh note quickly drowned by the twitter of other birds in the canopy and the gentle churring of insects. The stones led the party through the remnants of a broken gate. Ivy and lichens had long ago turned the wood to dirt, and time had reduced the hinges and locks to rust. As she passed, Fox touched one. The lock crumbled and left a smear of red across her palm.

On the other side of the gate stood hundreds of altars of stacked stone, row upon row like jagged teeth in a yawning green mouth, and at the center, a temple looming like hungry tongue from the earth.

"I have returned my brothers." Alavanja pressed past them, Hawthorne hot on the old man's heels. They grabbed the rusted iron ring on the great temple doors and the two men threw their weight into the effort. Slowly the door creaked open, vines of ivy falling in heaps around their feet.

The air in the temple pricked cold against Fox's skin. She rubbed the back of her neck, lying flat the hairs that had risen with the sudden temperature change. Maybe it was the quiet, the lack of bird calls, nothing except the occasional drone of bees, that had Fox on edge.

A white door untouched by the encroaching wilderness stood behind a broken altar. With a heavy exhale, Alavanja lowered himself onto one of the stone pieces. Fox peered at the old man. All of his earlier pep had abandoned him in a rush, like air from a balloon. Wrinkled skin clung to his skeleton as though his bones were all that kept him from melting into the moss-covered floor. "That is the way," Alavanja raised a bony finger toward the door. "The path can only be walked by a high priest, but I'm too old to make the journey. You must bring the **Marscon** to me." He peered up at his young apprentice, sadness blanketing his expression.

Hawthorne nodded, steeling himself. "I'll bring it back to you."

"There are traps and dangers, my boy." Alavanja said.

Fox strode to the doors. "That's what you hired me for," she said. Her fingers had just skimmed the glimmering stone when gears clicked like a winding clock. Fox jumped back as the doors swung outward. Frigid air rushed into the sanctuary from the yawning blackness beyond, raising goosebumps across Fox's skin.

"I dare not tread into the sanctum," said Jori, taking a seat on the other half of the broken alter next to Alavanja. The guide folded his arms across his chest.

"You stay, I lead them." Erskine spoke with unearned authority and halted any objection by disappearing into the dark tunnel.

"I think we'd better go after him," said Hawthorne with a wry smile.

Fox rolled her eyes then lit the lantern. Shouldering her small bag, she led Hawthorne as the two set off after the barbarian.

The lantern threw long shadows along the vaulted ceiling of the narrow passageway, illuminating silver wall sconces, their candles long burnt away and useless. In the dim, Fox could just make out mosaics of the old gods and their deeds. She touched the wall, feeling smooth bits of expertly laid tile that created the artwork.

"Fox, I've something I want to say," said Hawthorne after a few moments.

The realization of his sudden proximity in the semi-darkness sent a tremor across Fox's skin. She licked her lips, willing saliva back into her suddenly parched throat. "Out with it then."

"I know what you are." Hawthorne was close enough that his breath tickled against her ear lobe.

Fox turned, her back pressed against the tiles, the coolness seeping through her shirt. The light played on Hawthorne's features, accentuating the scar on his cheek and the wicked look in his eyes. Fox stuffed down the free-fall of fear icing her veins.

With a movement too quick to see, Hawthorne drew Fox's dagger from its sheath. Fox cursed herself for letting him get that close.

"I know what you are," said Hawthorne repeated, turning the weapon over in his hands, inspecting it by the light of the lantern.

Fox held her breath. If he knew about her magic, about her animal form…she hated the lengths she might need to go to keep the secret.

Hawthorne thumbed the dagger blade, testing the sharpness. "You're a thief."

Fox made a non-committal noise.

"Planning to double crossing us?" Hawthorne asked, admiring the dagger's hilt.

"If I said no would you believe me?" Fox let out a controlled exhale.

"Who was that silver-haired girl I saw you with in Jori's village? The dark skinned one?"

Fox narrowed her eyes. He'd followed her. She could've asked him the same thing of the man at the ale house, but she held her tongue. The two had been careful to stay in the shadows and Fox had never seen the other's face. "Careful with those skills or someone might think you're more than an old man's apprentice," said Fox levelly.

Hawthorne closed the infinitesimal gap between them, close enough that he'd be able to see the amber hued freckles dusted across her pale skin. "You have no idea." The dagger flashed in the light.

Fox sucked in her breath and screwed her eyes shut, expecting steel to open her throat. She heard a slight crunch, like stiff paper being folded, and opened her eyes.

Hawthorn held her dagger, a fat black spider on the tip, its legs wriggling madly. He scraped the arachnid off onto the wall with a squishy pop that left a streak of green goop and spider legs on the tiles.

"If you two done making the kissing faces, there is loud door." Fox smelled Erskine before he reached the patch of light thrown off by the lantern. The barbarian scowled at them, his great bushy brows two angry catapillars above his dark eyes.

Hawthorne handed Fox her weapon back, hilt first. She swiped the flat of the blade on her pants, removing creepy crawly remnants before sheathing the dagger. Fox ground her teeth together in irritation, enraged at herself for allowing Hawthorne to distract her. "Let's go," She pushed past the two men and continued down the sloping tunnel.

They moved deeper below the temple and Fox stopped.

"Why'd you stop?" Hawthorne narrowly avoided walking into her.

Erskine harrumphed his displeasure. "I said door loud."

"Do you hear that?" asked Fox. A faint droning sound filled the passage. Curiosity piqued, she walked forward. The noise grew louder and louder until Fox could feel the air vibrating with it. A few moments more brought the three to a wooden door and the sound to an almost deafening level.

Fox tested the knob. It turned easily, but the door didn't open. She threw her weight against it and the door didn't budge, stuck fast to its frame.

"Stand aside." Erskine took hold of the knob and pushed the door with his shoulder. The hinges creaked, and the wood splintered slightly, but it remained shut. "I try again." The barbarian backed up a few paces, took a running start and slammed into the door. splinters of wood clattered against the stone floor, but the damage was not enough to remove the obstacle. "One more try." Erskine backed up farther.

Fox flattened herself on the wall next to Hawthorne allowing the barbarian more

room to cannonball into the busted door.
"This is ridiculous," she muttered
flitting her hand to shoo away a couple of
bees. "Oh no, stop!" It was too late.

Erskine vaulted past her, ramming the
door at full speed. It exploded inward and
Fox grabbed Hawthorn's arm, pulling him to
the floor with her. She barely had time to
cover her head before the tunnel filled
with a mob of enraged bees. Erskine let
out a terrified bellow and sprinted
forward through the black buzzing cloud of
insects. His screams faded into the
distance until the only sound was frenzied
buzzing.

Fox lay on her stomach, her arms
trapping her breath against her face. She
waited. And waited more until the bees'
drone calmed. "Are you okay? Did you get
stung?" Fox's voice seemed too loud
compared to the earlier racket.

"No." Came the muffled reply.

"Follow me," said Fox, crawling on her
belly to the broken door. She touched the
remnants of the wood and her fingers sank

into a viscous fluid. Fox brought her hand to her face and sniffed. Then tentatively licked. Fox stood up slowly and relit the lantern. She looked up. The cavern roof was covered in beeswax stalactites, honey dripping from them in slow golden ribbons. The bees seemed now wholly unconcerned that their home had been broken into.

"Where is Erskine?" asked Hawthorne.

Fox shrugged her shoulders and inspected the cavern. She wondered how long the bees had lived here, centuries probably. Another tunnel opened on the other side of the beehive. As she approached, a heady bitter scent replaced the sweetness of honey. A flash of brass caught her attention. Fox held the lantern close to inspect it. A square panel fitted with a dial mechanism lay flush with the stone wall. With a quick flick of her finger, she easily moved the switch from one side of the dial to the other. Something deeper in the temple clicked and whirred as lanterns lining the passageway flared to life.

"Well then," murmured Hawthorn from behind her.

Fox doused the lantern and secured the handle to a loop on her small pack. They had not been walking long when the corridor veered sharply left. The rank of the barbarian made her nostrils flare.

"Are you alright, Erskine?" Fox turned the corner and halted. Erskine's body, barely recognizable, was inches from her face. His features were swollen and blistered by bee stings and it took a moment for Fox's brain to catch up to what her eyes saw. The barbarian's corpse was held aloft, like an over-stuffed scarecrow, by rows of iron spikes protruding from holes in the floor.

"It really is just you and me now, huh?" Hawthorne gulped.

"A trap," said Fox.

"Can we get past?"

"The spikes are wide enough that we can slip between them. Just don't step on the trigger," Fox gestured at the line of copper tiles just before the rows of spikes. A swath of them as wide as Erskine's boot were pushed a few centimeters lower than the others. She stepped over them and advanced forward. The stone floor felt solid under her boots and she wove a path between the spikes. Fox hopped over another row of copper tiles bordering the floor on the other side.

She heard a click and turned just in time to grab Hawthorne's collar and yank him out of harm's way. The entire stone slab beneath the spikes pivoted on a copper drum, Erskine's body slid into a black pit as he and the spikes disappeared leaving a flat surface behind. "You stepped on the tiles." Fox pushed Hawthorne roughly ahead of her into the corridor.

"The traps not going to re-spring itself," said Hawthorne defensively, pulling his shirt collar back into its proper place.

"It will if you reset it." Fox huffed.

"That's why we hired a thief." He said dryly.

Before long, the walls began to lose their smooth quality as pieces of rock jutted into the path. Thankfully, there were no more sudden turns, but they encountered another obstacle. A pit yawned before them, too far to jump across. Fox peered over the edge, a sheer cliff that dropped into absolute blackness. "This is inconvenient." She kicked a pebble, expecting to hear the chink of the rock hitting the bottom or a splash, but...nothing.

"Fox," Hawthorne said. He stood a bit away from her, a rope in his hand.

Fox's gaze followed the rope up to the ceiling where it was tied to a beam of rock. "Will it hold us?"

Hawthorne gave the rope a sharp tug. "Only one way to know." He took a running start and leapt onto the rope, letting the momentum carry him to the other side. His boots thudded softly against the ground when he landed. Turning, Hawthorne sent the rope back over the pit.

Fox caught it easily and gave it a few test tugs before getting a running start. She white knuckled the rope, her stomach dropping into her knees with the weightless sensation. Air whooshed past her and she resisted the urge to shut her eyes as she swung over the bottomless chasm. Hawthorne caught her, holding the rope above her head. Bile rose to the back of Fox's tongue, bitter at the thought that he only needed let go and she would plummet to her death in the dark abyss.

Fox muttered a prayer of thanks when her feet hit solid ground and she scrubbed her fingers on her pants legs, relieving them of the ache of holding on too tightly.

"You don't like heights?" Hawthorne asked nonchalantly.

"I don't like falling from them." Fox snatched the rope from him and secured the end on one of the rocks.

"What's so important about this thing your master wants?" Fox asked, the two of them moving deeper along the path. Nicklaus had told her enough about the **Marscon** that Fox hadn't found it necessary to listen to Alavanja's mutterings around the campfire every night.

"Alavanja is not my master. He's a teacher," said Hawthorne gruffly. Their path turned into a winding staircase.

"Sorry. Your teacher, why does he want it?" She asked mounting the narrow steps.

"There's an ancient race, the Theafisians, supposedly very advanced. Their empire reached across all the continents. According to the legends, they had some sort of great power that was a combination of machine and magic that could slaughter thousands in the blink of an eye. Alavanja thinks that this **Marscon** holds the key to that power."

"Nice bedtime story. You didn't say why he wants it," she said. People seeking power worried her.

"He's the last high priest of Theafis," Hawthorne said.

"Explains why he's so old."

"Can you imagine what someone would pay to possess the kind of power contained in this relic?" Hawthorne chuckled low in his throat, the sound more growl than laugh.

"Money would make getting magically blown up more tolerable." Fox threw him a look over her shoulder.

The corners of Hawthorne's lips turned up in amusement. "Paying attention for traps?" He asked, voice oozing charm.

Fox's heart flipped into her throat. "Don't distract me."

"Why do they call you Fox?" Hawthorne asked.

"Because it's my name." She scoffed.

"Is it a nickname or something? If you're not looking for traps and we both die. I don't think my life would be complete."

"Do you have a death wish?" Fox asked. She wondered how high into the structure the stairs lead. If she'd gone on this treasure hunt alone, she might've taken a moment or two to marvel at the intricate construction of the temple and the endless vault within.

"I'm making conversation. If you don't want to tell me, *fine.* I don't really care."

Fox sighed audibly. "Sterling Fox. What's yours?"

"Hawthorne Luck. It sounds like a good pirate's name. Don't you think? You'd make a good pirate," said Hawthorne. "You've already got the thief part down. And hey, we're looking for treasure."

"I'm not interested in being a pirate. And we're not looking for a chest full of jewels." Something about the turn of the conversation had Fox thinking she should be wary of the apprentice.

"Same difference," said Hawthorne.

The stairs opened into a large circular chamber. The gods here were carved into the walls, their mouths all agape as though surprised by the intrusion into their sanctum. At the room's center there was a white stone altar like the broken one in the temple's main room with a small black statue on top.

Fox approached the altar and looked closely at the figure. A round head with large eyes and antennae atop a rounder body. The small god, no bigger than the height of Fox's hand, had four arms, three of which wrapped around his hefty belly. The fourth arm, the tiny god raised in salutation. Fox tilted her head. The figurine was reminiscent of a bumble bee, but without wings, making it alien to her. Tiny cracks had formed over the surface of the black clay statue.

"Is it safe to take?" Hawthorne asked. He hadn't ventured very far into the room.

Fox shrugged and snatched the statue from its place. She froze, waiting. Nothing happened. Slowly she exhaled and tucked the statue into her pack. Her foot was on the topmost stair when thunder rocked through them. Torrents of water exploded from the open mouths of the gods.

"Go." She shoved Hawthorne toward the stairs.

They ran, the flood on their heels. Fox slipped on the bottom stair, feeling her lantern and pack crunch under her. She twisted trying to regain her footing and her bag slipped from her shoulder, the water pushing her forward. Hawthorne grabbed her hand and pulled her to her feet. He scooped her pack up from the wet floor and shoved it in her direction. The pit loomed ahead. "We'll have to go together." Hawthorne's words were barely audible over the rush of water behind them. He grabbed the rope.

Fox gripped the rope and screwed her eyes shut as they sailed over the empty blackness. Her heart leapt into her throat. She opened her eyes as the swing jerked, Hawthorn was holding the rope just above her head. "Sorry," he said and let go. Fox felt her body falling backwards.

She held on, her palms burning. Her stomach lurched and she bit down on the terrified scream sliding across her tongue. Anger burned inside her chest as the rope swung back and forth, slowly losing momentum, until it stopped.

Hawthorne stood on the side of the pit, tossing the statue from hand to hand. "I have to thank you, Sterling Fox." He smirked.

Fox narrowed her eyes. His once enticing smile now made rage bubble inside of her chest.

"We've been trying to get this for a long time."

"You and Alavanja can rot," spit Fox.

Hawthorne snorted derisively. "Alavanja was just a means to an end. This is pirate treasure, Sterling." He turned and disappeared down the tunnel.

Mist from the water falling over one side of the pit touched Fox's skin. She doubted that there would be enough water down there that would allow her to let go and swim to the other side. Her arms quivered from the effort of not falling to her death. She looked up at the beam far above her head and began to climb.

Fox reached the top and pulled herself on the flat rock. From this new angle she could see that the rocks sticking out from the wall formed a set of stairs, one side leading to each side of the pit. A laugh escaped her, the sound that coming out of her mouth more like a shriek than a laugh and it echoed from the walls.

She descended the stairs, careful of her footing and continued the trek out of the temple. A low moan drifted down the path toward her. Fox approached cautiously; the iron spikes had been triggered. A sly smile eased itself onto Fox's face. "Well, this is fortuitous." She wove her way through the iron bars until she stood above the prone Hawthorne.

He was twisted and stretched, having attempted to escape the deadly barbs. One spike caught him through the shin, shattering the bone and shredding the muscle. Bits of his tibia lay scattered across the stone slab. His fingers stretched toward the row of copper tiles on the other side of the slab but remained just out of his reach. Hawthorne's breath came out slow and shallow.

Fox rummaged through Hawthorne's bag and took the **Marscon**. She tamped down the ache of guilt in her stomach. He'd tried to double-cross her, but not just her, the entire organization she worked for. Leaving him here would be a mercy compared to the tortures that the collector would device.

Hawthorne's hand on her ankle stopped her. "Please don't leave me." His beautiful baritone cracked with pain.

Fox muttered a curse and weighed her options. A dead man was never good for one's conscience. "Take off your belt." She ordered.

Hawthorne's scream vibrated against the walls when she tightened the tourniquet on his thigh.

"Both hands." Fox grabbed him by the wrists and held fast. She stepped on the copper tiles. They sank under her weight and the disk began to turn. Hawthorne's leg fell free of the spike and Fox pulled, throwing her body into the movement.

They tumbled backwards onto solid ground as the slab clicked into place. Fox helped Hawthorne to his good foot, letting him lean on her for support. They hobbled back through the beehive and collected the lantern.

Despite the extra weight and the slow shuffle up hill, their trek to the entrance of the temple seemed shorter than the descent. Fox nudged the door open wider and stepped into the main chamber.

"Take Lucky back to the ship," said a cloaked man standing a short distance away. She recognized it as the same cloak that Hawthorne had worn the day he came into Nicklaus's shop.

Fox's eyes flew open, her gaze darting around the temple. A half a dozen armed men occupied the place. Jori and Alavanja were not among them, but she saw their packs had been gutted, supplies strewn across the ground.

"You really are a pirate." Fox said to Hawthorne as two other men carried him. Before they took him through the doors, Hawthorne smiled cockily. One of the men bumped Hawthorne's leg, and the sinister expression disappeared in a howl of pain.

"What happened to Erskine?" The cloaked man approached Fox.

"He's dead," said Fox.

"Pity." The cloaked man stalked back and forth in front of her for a moment, seeming to evaluate her. "My brother was right. You are a pretty thief." He pushed back his hood.

Fox froze.

A mirror reflection of Hawthorne stared at her. Same stormy eyes, same lips twisted in a half smile, but his scar was on the opposite side of his face. "Captain Percival Luck," he introduced himself with an almost flamboyant bow. "Now, give me the treasure." He growled.

A rook cried out, the gaveled quark echoing off the temple walls.

Fox removed her pack and tossed it at Captain Luck, who caught it with ease. He pulled the **Marscon** from it and turning it over to inspect it in the light, laughed. "Very good," he said. "You'd make a fine pirate."

"Your brother said the same thing."

The sharp whisper of crossbow bolts lit the air. One bolt struck Captain Luck in the hand and he dropped the **Marscon**. Fox lunged for the statue. She hit the ground, her knee taking the brunt of the impact as the warm black clay fell into her palm. Rolling away from the pirate, she clambered back to her feet. Another bolt whistled next to her ear, striking one of the men behind her. He stumbled backwards in surprise and fell to the ground.

Fox sprinted through the temple door and past the yawning altars inside. Chancing a glance over her shoulder, she saw the silver-haired head of Tevan, bobbing close behind and the angry faces of pirates chasing after them both. The two women veered away from the path of columns, crashing through the forest.

Ignoring the slap of leaves and sapling branches against her body as she hurtled through the underbrush, Fox ran as fast as her human legs would carry her.

Tevan turned, fired another two rounds from her automatic crossbow at their pursuants. "Split," she hollered, turning sharply right, crashing through the greenery. A puff of black smoke and her Rook form shot out of the other side, a caw from its beak, wings beating, carrying it into the canopy.

Fox twisted left, her eyes searching for cover. The men chasing her gained ground, their shouts ringing louder in her ears. Fox bit hard into the statue, the black clay warming her lips and tongue. She leapt forward into the dense thicket. Her skin seared white hot as magic crackled in her ears. Fox scurried further into thicker into the bushes and wrapped her furry body around the precious treasure. She waited.

Breathless seconds passed before the pirates came crashing through the forest. One stopped, his boot close enough to Fox's face that she could've bit him without much effort.

"Where'd they go?" Bellowed the large bald one.

"Keep Looking," said the other.

They were looking for a redheaded thief, not a small red fox. The pirates moved off. With the statue in her maw, Fox cautiously crawled from her hiding place. Thinking it best to keep her animal form for a while, she made her way through the forest. It wasn't long before Tevan, in her rook form, found her. The black bird flew from bush to bush, leading the red fox to the small clearing where she'd landed her airship.

Fox broke into a run. Her paws touched on the steel gangplank and she summoned her magic, emerging from a cloud of black smoke as her human self.

She spit the statue into her hand and flexed her lower jaw, swallowing the dirty taste of clay, working out the tension in her cheeks. Behind her, Tevan emerged from her own puff of smoke. "I am glad you're safe." Tevan threw her arms around Fox and pulled her into a tight hug. She kissed Fox's face feverishly, forehead, cheeks, and lips.

Fox smiled against the soft kiss. "I'm alright, thanks to you." She stepped back and pulled the leaver to bring the gangplank inside. The airship's door closed with a soft hiss of air.

"I brought the others on board. And by the time I got back for you, the pirates were already there." Tevan said as they walked up the ramp to the bridge.

Fox opened the metal door and the faces of Alavanja and Jori peered at her. Teevan took her place, gears and machinery humming happily under the bird woman's touch. Fox slid into her place behind the communications console, now realizing how much she'd missed it after several weeks away chasing the small god in her hand.

"I tried to lose the pirates in the forest," said Jori from where he sat behind her.

"It's okay." Fox was glad to have an explanation for the winding route through the forest and a new respect for the guide. "We'll return you to your village."

"If it's all the same, I will stay with you." Jori said.

Fox quirked an eyebrow.

Jori crossed his arms over his chest and nodded as though Fox had no choice but to allow that.

The airship lurched slightly as the balloon above began to inflate and the ship rose into the air. Fox peered through the side window at the swiftly shrinking trees. Soon the four of them were hidden in the clouds.

"Are we safe now?" Alavanja asked Tevan. His voice was quiet against the click and whir of the airship's mechanics.

"Relatively," she answered. "Nicklaus will want your journals."

The old man seemed resigned to the fact that he had never been in charge of the entire adventure. "May I just hold the **Marscon**? I've come all this way."

Fox and Tevan exchanged glances. Fox shrugged and handed the clay doll over, her palm cooled by the sudden absence of it.

"Would you like to know a secret?" Alavanja admiring the happy face of the small god with his wide eyes and welcoming smile. "This is a key that will unlock great power."

"Doesn't look it," said Tevan. Her dark fingers held onto the wheel, making minor corrections to keep the ship hidden in the troposphere.

Before anyone could stop him, Alavanja threw the statue hard against the metal plated floor. The black clay shattered, scattering like stars across the sky.

They all blinked. In the middle of the floor lay the largest gemstone Fox had ever seen. It was red in color with a slit of black at its center that reminded her of a cat's eye. A jeweler of great skill had set the perfectly cut stone inside of a delicate golden filigree that spidered out like nerves. The whole thing was larger than Fox's palm. She picked it up, feeling the white heat of magic trickling into her fingers and through the rest of her body.

She turned it over, inspecting it. "This is interesting."

The End?

Blaved: Only the Good Parts - Part 2

By Andrew Hiller

Earlier—

Margarine shimmied down a string of sticky vines that clung to the castle walls of Lumpadunk's castle like a tax collector's grip on a widow's last dollar. Swinging, she crossed over to a balcony before dropping farther down. Her spiked heels stabbed into the mortar between snow white bricks as her perfect lacquered nails searched for handholds. Inch by inch, she lowered herself, fearing the touch of the kingdom's infamous squealing ivy. She imagined an easier way, perhaps being strapped to the back of a protective, tireless giant, but alas, she was the hero and not the damsel.

Halfway down, her foot slipped, dainty ankle twisting in pain. A heel popped,

shattering like a glass slipper after a
ball. Scrabbling, she tried to find
purchase. It occurred to her in a moment
of freefall that descending down a castle
wall in high heels was the height... No... a
veritable cliff of insanity. Still, for
the sake of saving her true friend, she
thought, she would make any leap.

"Oof," Margarine oofed.

She landed in a brace of interlocking
branches that formed a thorny shrubbery to
the left of a barebacked, spotted
knabstrupper. The shrubbery's prickles
pinched her quite unforgivably. In her
pain, she disregarded the horse's whinny
of alarm though she pursed in lips in
annoyance at the realization that the
polka dotted black and white steed had
taken two long strides to avoid "catching"
her. This seemed an unchivalrous act for
such a noble breed of war horse.

*We must leap ahead again dear reader
unless you are eager to read a twelve-
hundred page diversion on Stemish horse
breeding practices, and how the*

knapstrupper, once thought to be of Danish origin, is in its current configuration, entirely Stemish. In short, the breed initially imported by the warlord, Portigal was interbred with the American Appaloosa. After some trial and error, this process produced the perfect night-time war steed. Opposing armies were completely befuddled by the impeccable camouflage of the Stemish kanpstrupper's black and white starry coats. In fact, the interbreeding worked so well that Stemish Knapstruppers are believed to be the only war horses in the world with spots that twinkle.

The knapstrupper snorted, shaking a face splotched as a tree used as a shield during a snowball fight. Margarine patted its flank reassuringly. Then, tore down the putrescent streets, hobbling on a sore ankle and only one heel.

Around several corners, and any number of long blocks, Margarine came upon a row of tenement houses. Here, the bustle of foot traffic disappeared except for the occasional interruption of "Psst Buddy!" and "Mind your own business or you'll get cut!"

About her, the numbers carved into rude pieces of wood marked the only difference between one building and the next. Each wreck of a house sagged in the middle, and wore a thatched roof that looked like a tweed coat in need of some good leather patches.

"Forty-one, thirty-eight, ninety-six," Margarine read with a pout. Annoyed that Lumpadunk was so cheap that he hired illiterate city planners. Any ordinary block would go in sequence, but not Stemish streets!

Sorry. We're going to jump ahead again for if you ever visited Stemland you know, as Margarine did not, that the first thing visitors do when they arrive is get lost and even the locals, helpful and generous as Stemmish citizens are, shrug when asked for directions, usually being lost themselves.

The reason for this, as Goldman points out in seventy-three concise pages, is rooted in a period called the Balsa Wars.

For a period of three hundred years, Stemland had been victimized by constant invasions. Their defenses broken down like... well balsa wood.

The perfect environment and unparalleled rolling Stemmish landscapes that make it far superior to any other land for strolling also made it tempting for armies who did not want to ford, surmount, or deal with any natural obstacles. Of course, the Stemish army would beat the invaders back, being the greatest army of any army that ever armed, but the invasions grew tiresome as they interrupted so many tea times.

"We must divert the enemy!" Henrick III declared, "We shall do so by creating false maps, so the enemy gets lost. Being so frustrated they will simply return home."

Thus, from that day no building in Stemland has been numbered in any relation to its peers... much to Margarine Snifter's frustration.

"Eleven thousand and seventy-three. Six. Twenty-four. Negative eighteen." Read Margarine with a sour expression. After an hour of searching, she was practically ready to return to Lumpadunk. When, in an off chance, she backtracked and found the undistinguished, cookie cutter tenement house of Mundane Min.

"Forty-two!" Margarine crowed. "Forty-two will be the answer to all my problems! To everything!"

She traipsed up the broken steps and pounded on the door, ignoring the knocker because the owner of the door had glued thumbtacks all about it.

"Go away!" A voice squeaked.

Margarine knocked again.

"Mundane Min!" she called out. Behind the door, Margarine heard a shuffling of feet and mumbling. An extra three sets of latches thudded into place.

"I need your help!"

"The check's in the mail. Check the debtor's prison. Go away!"

Margarine Snifter sighed. She took exactly one step to the right, jimmied her fingers under a window, raised a pane of glass, and climbed in.

Min, dressed in a white lab coat with oversized spectacles and something that looked like a reflective saucer hanging off her forehead, glared at Margarine Snifter. She picked up something round and heavy. The sixth most beautiful woman in the world raised her hands.

"Wait, Professor Amum. We've met before." Margarine said, ducking, "At the inventor's conference. I presented a vaccine and you..."

"I don't remember," Min growled, turning quickly to drape a pillowcase over a photograph of Min and Margarine clinking champagne filled test tubes.

"Min." Margarine implored.

Mundane Min jumped. Her white lab coat flapped open, revealing a Che Guevara T-shirt. It looked marvelous.

"Go away." she repeated, "Why would you ever want to work with a plagiarist? Someone who faked their data? Oh, what a circus! Oh, what a show!" she complained, "Haven't I faced enough derision? Enough mockery? Why don't you just leave a bag of flaming poop on my stoop! Who wants an invention from—"

"You were the best." Margarine patted a clockwork doorstopper on Min's shelf.

"I was fired from university. Lost my tenure. My wife left me for a chocolatier. She said at least sweets would make her disgrace go down easier."

"I know what Count Rougehand—"

"No one ever reads retractions. Go away."

"It's for a righteous cause. Lumpadunk with the help of Roguehand is trying to murder my true friend. Please. Help me save my friend."

"Fiend? You want me to save your fiend?" Min paused, then shook her head, "I'm a mundane scientist. Not a mad one. Go away."

"Friend. Friend! True Friend."

"One, two... Why would anyone need so many fiends in their life?"

"Friendship?"

"Fiendship?

"Isn't friendship important to you at all? Wouldn't you do anything for a true friend?"

"True friend?" the disgraced professor relented, putting a horn in her ear. "True friendships are rare. Rare as a well-done bison burger with habanero mayo with just the right squeeze of lime, but no... I can't help you... I just can't."

"If you help me, I can arrange a fellowship."

Mundane Min drummed her fingers against a distended lip. She paced in a short circle.

"No, not good enough. I'm forcibly retired."

"Revenge?" Margarine tried.

Mundane Min stopped. She raised a finger, then paced in short circles, her feet scuffing a carpet emblazoned with the periodic table.

"Revenge, you say?"

Margarine nodded.

"Against the three toed man?"

Margarine nodded again.

"The man who murdered my thesis? And stole my place as Lumpadunk's advisor?"

Margarine nodded a third time.

Mundane Min rubbed her hands together. A small smile unfolded.

"You know, I always wanted to go up to the three toed man and say, 'Hello. I am Min Amum. You murdered my reputation. Prepare for a rebuttal!"

"If you help me. He will suffer mortifications abundant!"

Margarine Snifter tented her fingers.

"Now, that's a worthy cause! What do you need?"

"A compass that points to my location no matter where in the world the holder is so that my true friend can always find me."

Min nodded several times.

"A Global Person Spotter?"

"Yes, I know it sounds impossible.... That it would take a miracle, but..."

"Hah!" Min huffed. If there was one thing Mundane Min didn't believe in it was miracles. She slapped her knee and began rummaging in her trunk. With a bark of triumph, she removed a pair of plyers and yanked off a lock of Margarine Snifter's hair before magnetizing it. Then, she began dumping solutions into various vats and turning on all her Bunsen Burners. Liquid evaporated and steamed through coils of tubing. A spark of electricity danced across the room along thin metal rods.

Mundane Min rubbed her hands together.

"Impossible? Ha! Shows what you know! It's only mostly impossible. When something's really impossible there's only one thing to do—"

"Put it on the Home Shopping Network as a miracle cure?"

Mundane Min eyed her. Then, she waved off any response, "No. What you ask is only practically impossible. With practically impossible..." Min fiddled with a bellows and a wad of caramel, explaining. "The melting sugars help the impossible deal with being shown up."

Soon, the room was alive with bubbling, fizzing, smoking, shaking, exploding, and vibrating activity. Min's tendency to break out into spontaneous laughter unnerved Margarine a bit. The sixth most beautiful woman in the world glanced at a sweating grandfather clock. Chemical condensation slicked its oak sideboards.

"Um..." Margarine Snifter, interrupted.

Mundane Min rushed past her with a box of loadstones.

"Um..." Margarine Snifter sniffed. Min paused. Ooze expanding from the tip of her ballpoint pen.

"Will all this inventing take long? I have to return to the castle before I'm missed."

Mundane Min gave Margarine a most serious look.

"Never rush a scientist." She declared, hammering a spring straight with a ballpeen mallet, "You rush a scientist you get crack pot inventions

Margarine stared out the window, fearing to see the signs of marching troops, the sound of trumpets announcing the discovery of her absence.

"I... uh." Margarine said.

Min lifted her spectacles, revealing eyes newly aglitter. A puff of smoke issued from a tea kettle.

"Go on. Go on." Min said, dismissing her. "Come back tomorrow and I'll have your Global Person Spotter... your GPS."

"Thank you." Margarine hesitated. It felt wrong to leave without helping, but Min shooed her away, shoving her out the door.

"Get going, Margarine. Have fun climbing the castle."

FireLight

by Luna Nyx Frost

For humans, our fire burns
internally with passion and desire.
In nature, fire burns chemically
spontaneously and uncontrollable.

Our hearts and spirit are what light
the kindling of our ambitions and dreams.
Our passion, is consumed with a white
blaze
consumed with the need to make our dreams
a reality.

Regardless, of the cost or the sacrifices
made.
Fueled by our emotions and thoughts
painting our world in a sea of red

Forcing us to lash out with
our fists or barbaric words,
creating a chain reaction,

Rogues and Rebels

a human forest fire.

Until the red-hot coals of anger burn out
Leaving the bitter feelings
of self-loathing and regret
For your sins, we created
in our own desperate need
to put out our flames?

What is the difference then?
Between our soul fire and the wild
bush fires found in nature?
Are they both not simple flames
consuming everything they touch
creating unique chaos in its wake.

Or is there something more
to its hypnotic dance?
Our eternal flame leading us astray
Waiting for the solitary spark
To ignite into an eternal blaze.

The Sea Witch

By Luna Nyx Frost

Humans always wonder
what life is like beneath the waves?
Dreaming of a magical world
full of merfolk.

Oh, how delusional humans can be,
not realizing how alike we are.
Men in control while women
bow to their every whim.

Rebellion leads to isolation
and the loss of a throne.
Forced to hide in the depths of the sea
becoming the mermaids boogeyman.

People cowering away from you in fear,
seeing you as nothing more than a monster.
Misunderstanding magic
seeing it as another form of evil.

Yet, desperation leads fools to my
doorstep,
seeking spells for quick fixes and happy
endings.
Expecting these miracles for free
not comprehending that
a payment must always be made.

Why must I be denied this same
arrangement?
Rejected the opportunity of reclaiming my
throne.
Even with my magic and aid to those below,
they will never see me as a royal
just a hag forever trapped under the
waves.

Rat

By Tempie W. Wade

"I demand to be released!" screamed Wilson, pulling at the ropes that bound his hands behind his back. "I am a Captain in the service of the Crown. You cannot treat me this way!" He attempted to move his feet, but they were tied, as well, and it left him lying on his side, uncomfortable, his cheek on the damp, musty floor of the cell he had been dumped in earlier that morning. Trying to lift his head, the wretched reek of urine from a bucket—used for the previous prisoner's 'needs'—assaulted his senses, causing bile to rise in the back of his throat. He managed to wiggle his body around to avoid the stench as best he could. Once settled, he blew out a long breath, going over the events of the day in his mind, trying to make some sense of it all.

One minute he was enjoying his morning coffee with a bite to eat, and the next, his door was busted down and he was taken into custody. Two of his fellow soldiers held him against the wall as three more searched his home, destroying everything as they went, even going so far as to tear open the mattress on his bed. He watched them, confused and concerned, as they went outside with a leather bundle of papers he had never seen before.

"What are you doing?" he demanded. "You cannot come in here like this!"

"I can do whatever I need to do to root out the traitors in our midst," he heard a voice say.

He snapped his head around to see that bastard John André smirking back at him from the front of the house.

"I am no traitor!" he growled.

André looked down at the parchments he had just been handed. "These letters from General Washington say differently." He stepped closer. "How long have you been spying for him? I can't say that it surprises me, but what meant so much to you that you felt the need to betray your king and country? What did he give you in return?"

"I have no idea what you are talking about."

"Major André," said one of the men, handing him a burlap bag. "We found this in the bottom of a trunk beneath his bed. I think you will be interested in what it contains."

"Well, let's see what we have here," he opened the bag, rummaging around until he settled on one piece. He reached in, producing a bracelet that he held up by the clasp. "Would you like to explain what you are doing with the personal jewelry of a woman who was kidnapped very recently? One that the British army had to pay a substantial ransom to get back safely and one whose husband gave you a thorough thrashing not that long ago? Trying to get a little payback, were you?"

"I have never seen that before in my life."

André chuckled. "I am sure her items just magically appeared under your bed, along with those letters from the enemy camp that were sewn up in your mattress." He stepped closer. "One little piece of advice; the first thing you learn in intelligence is to always burn the letter and dispose of the evidence so that it cannot be traced back to you, but of course, no one ever accused you of being smart." André looked to the men. "Take him to the gaol. We will be along to interrogate him shortly."

"You cannot do this André!" he shoved one of the men to the side, attempting to get his hands on the Major, but he was tackled to the floor and held with his cheek flat against the it as André crouched down.

"I am merely doing my job; however, I *have* been feeling rather poorly lately, so I think I may need to recruit a volunteer to help question you, and I have to say, I would not want to be in your boots when he arrives."

Wilson's thoughts were interrupted when he heard the rattle of a key in the door. He attempted to sit up as three familiar men entered the cell.

Major John André was accompanied by the leader of the Queen's Rangers, Lt. Colonel Simcoe and that damn Scotsman, the man he had thrown in the very same gaol cell for beating him senseless...Duncan MacGregor. The trio stood in front of him, all looking rather pleased with the circumstances. MacGregor's jaw was clenched, and he opened and closed his fists, seemingly anxious to get on with it.

"I don't know what you think you are doing ,André," said Wilson, pushing up on his side only to fall back over "but I have done nothing wrong and if anything happens to me, you will pay the price." Wilson chuckled, somewhat insanely. "Are you going to beat a man with his hands and feet tied? Make sure you put that in your report to General Clinton. It will reflect so nicely upon on you."

Simcoe turned to MacGregor. "What say you? If we untie him, do you think you can keep him from escaping, by any means necessary?"

"Aye! Gladly!" he replied.

Simcoe shrugged, and moved over to cut Wilson loose.

Wilson stumbled to his feet, rubbing his wrists before raking his hair back from his face. "Did you do this MacGregor? Plant evidence in my home to pay me back for putting you in here?"

André leaned against the door of the cell. "He doesn't answer your questions; you answer mine."

"Fuck off, MAJOR!" he shouted, spitting at him. "I have nothing to say to the likes of you."

André smiled. "I was hoping that would be your answer."

An hour later, the three men departed, leaving Wilson lying on the floor, blood spilling from his mouth and nose. He was fairly certain he had a few cracked ribs and his face hurt like hell, but he was alive, and surprised that MacGregor had left him among the living. There could only be one reason for that--they planned to torture him further, and for information he did not have, because he had not betrayed his country and he sure as hell wouldn't do anything that helped that bastard traitor Washington.

Wilson stretched out on his side and laughed, his gaze focused in on a rather large rat that had appeared in the corner, seemingly eyeing him and sizing him up. The creature must have caught the smell of fresh blood, because its nose twitched as if it were a familiar—and enticing—scent.

Rats could be nasty; the filthy beasts carried all sorts of diseases and one bite from the right one could painfully end a man's life. Of course, one bite of a rat from a man, could end the rat's life, depending on which one had the bigger desire to live at that time.

Wilson decided, in that moment, that no matter what happened, he would be the rat that survived, and the ones that had wronged him would pay the ultimate price, no matter how long it might take.

Blaved: Only the Good Parts - Part 3

By Andrew Hiller

As Margarine and the Man in Corduroy stepped onto the gangplank of the Good Ship Sacrifice, a blossoming rose sunset blinded them. They shaded their eyes and gazed at beams of ruby, burgundy, pink, and ordinary red tinted beams, rails, and admired the sparkling waves. A purser accepted their tickets, noting with a raised eye that the pair opted for separate rooms. Margarine shared a joke and her companion laughed and pointed. The boat bobbed beneath them as even great boats are wont to do. Neither cared. Both knew that after all their trials no sea could upset the bonds of their friendship. The Man in Corduroy patted Margarine on the back secure that in the history of the world there were only three remarkable friendships that time had bronzed and put on its bookshelf as a keepsake and theirs would—

"Hold it!" the editor cried out, eyes crinkling with suspicion, "Is this a buddy book?" She slammed a hand on the red lined pages she'd been reviewing.

"Uh…" the author spluttered.

"Where's the romance! After all the Man in Corduroy did for Margarine how could she not love him? It wouldn't be fair. Why would you even submit this to me!"

"Well," the author blushed, "Someday, you might not mind buddy books so much!"

Author and editor stared one another down. The author, as always, blinked first.

"I…"

"You promised me a story with everything!" the editor accused, "Thrills, escapes, duels, explosions, schemes, inventions, magic, giants, dragons, aardvarks!"

"I did," the author confessed.

"Well, how can a story have everything if it doesn't have love?"

The author thought. He tapped his thigh, twirling through his mental rolodex for just the right phrase, but spoken words are not the province of authors. They are like **Mars, con**trary and thin of oxygen. A place where the gravity never feels quite right. Better, thought the author, to rove in the fields of curiosity and opportunity for years hunting for the right expression than to rush out a lame repost. Demanding a spontaneous eloquence? Ridiculous, he stamped, a writer must range near and far just to find a sign that hopefully doesn't shout, "Yield," "Stop," or "Duck Crossing!"

The editor thwacked the author on the head with a ruler, realizing that he, once again, had become distracted.

"But," the author tried, shuffling his feet. "Not every man and woman who meet must fall in love. There are many types of love."

"And what happens to the fiancé?" the editor said, clearly not satisfied.

"Lumpadunk?"

She nods.

"He lives and gets his tulips."

"Gah!"

"But..."

The editor threw up her hands. "What? What kind of story is this?"

"Look," the author placated, "I can see you're getting upset. Maybe we should stop and return to these pages when you are feeling better."

The editor turned red as her favorite pen's bloody ink. With an angry yank, she popped the cork on a bottle of Stemish wine and downed the entire bottle in one swig. Its thick rustic earthiness soothed her. The author had been edging towards the door, but she motioned him back. He paused. Then, she pushed the manuscript across her hinge-paneled Lieseuse desk.

"It needs some revision," she said.

The author's eyes rounded. "It looks... um.. thinner."

"I had to cut a bit."

The author flipped through the pages. More than twelve thousand pages had been red-lined. A look of horror grew on his face.

"Where's…" he said, alarmed, "And there's no…" he said, aghast, "But what about the…" he stuttered, "And does the story even work without a two-hundred-page explanation of…"

\#

Margarine stuck out her perfect hand. The Man in Corduroy took it. He grasped it tightly. She pumped it heartily three times. History records only three world changing handshakes: Edison and Ford, C.S. Lewis and J. R. R. Tolkien, and Laverne and Shirley, but this one… well, this one had all the love of the world.

124

The Polar Star

By Allison Norfolk

December 1928. St. Paul, Minnesota

"Have you ever been to one of these racing tracks before?" Tank asked.

"No," said Tinker, pulling her gaze from the city view zipping by through the frosted glass of the high-speed trolley window. "My best friend Minerva has been a few times, though. She says the races are very exciting. I never saw the point, though. It's just dogs running in a circle for a few seconds."

She noticed with some amusement that several other pairs of eyes around the trolley became very interested in looking everywhere but at her and her companion. Both Tinker and Tank had grown used to this reaction whenever they went out in public; while people probably had read in the papers about the mutilated war hero whose entire outer shell was a fabricated prosthetic, it was another to be confronted with a seven-foot metal man doing something so absurdly normal as riding the trolley.

Tinker was also aware that seated next to him, her wiry pale frame made him look even larger and more intimidating by comparison. She'd striven to the best of her ability to humanize his silver body and give him a nonthreatening design with as many smooth edges as she could manage without making him clownish. He even had a face, though it lacked expression beyond the attempt at a smile she'd painstakingly enameled to cover the rounded radio speaker from which his voice emerged. There was nothing she could do about his size; the components that allowed him to speak were in part constructed from a cannibalized piano and required a certain amount of internal space to work properly.

Of course, what people didn't know was exactly how little of Tank's original human body remained—that is to say, none at all. His soul alone was encased in the metal humanoid body Tinker had built for him. It was his lifeforce that provided the spark that animated the suit, though the body itself, like all prosthetic limbs, was largely powered on self-sustaining kinetic energy, stored as it moved. When they first met, his soul was trapped powering a rusting hulk of a tank from the Great War, and he had no memory of who he had been before that. Their quest to discover Tank's origins had brought them to the attention of the Federal government in a bad way—and the aftermath of that encounter left them in debt to St. Paul's motley organized crime network.

And it was that which brought them here today.

Tinker glanced around the high-speed trolley. "I think our stop is next."

It was the middle of the morning, so they were the only ones to exit at the trolley stop closest to the track. The races wouldn't be until seven or eight o'clock, after most people got off shift for the day. Tinker felt the stares of their fellow passengers follow them through the trolley windows even after they exited and started making their way up the platform to towards the street. Then the trolley rose up on its magnetic levitation wheels and shot off down the gleaming silver single track line towards its next destination.

They were alone.

The racetrack was a big enough draw to warrant its own trolley stop, and since the complex was only a few years old, the station was new as well. Unlike most older stations, this one was entirely indoors to protect the crowds from Minnesota's harsh winters. The walls were decorated with stylized relief designs, black lacquered backgrounds with golden greyhounds and mother-of-pearl stars. The dogs' long, tapered noses were all pointed in the direction of the covered tunnel walkway that led straight into the racetrack complex.

"At least they leave us no doubt about where to go," remarked Tinker. Her voice echoed in the empty station, as did the heavy chinks of Tank's footfalls against the dark marble floors.

As they walked, she took a moment to smooth out a semi-imagined wrinkle in her skirt. While she was currently dressed as a respectable young woman in a green dress, fitted black coat, white gloves and a small green hat perched on her cropped blonde hair, normally she was to be found in her machinist's workshop covered in rust and grease stains, wearing her older brother's castoffs. It always took her a little while to get used to the feel of a skirt against her thighs again.

Past the stiles where their trolley tickets were punched, the entrance to the track was barred by a heavy iron folding gate decorated with swooping, graceful curves in the abstract outline of yet more greyhounds. It was securely locked and rattling it produced no result, but Tinker discovered a small button bearing the label next to it 'Deliveries.' She pressed it.

A pleasant chime sounded in the distance. A minute later Tank said, "Someone's coming."

Sure enough, not long afterwards Tinker's less sensitive human ears also picked up two sets of footfalls: one booted, the other scratching paws.

A lean man with graying temples and weathered skin appeared on the far side of the iron gate. In contrast to the opulent surroundings, he wore long dark trousers and a long-sleeved collared wool shirt and dusty leather boots—obviously work clothes rather than anything meant to impress. At his side, tied to his beltloop by a loose leather thong fastened to a collar about its neck, trotted a beautiful creamy-golden greyhound, a match for the relief ones in the trolley station.

The man did a double take when he saw Tank. He stopped about a pace behind the gate and sized up the pair of them. "Can I...help you?" he asked finally.

"Yes. We're here to speak to Mr. Croxton," said Tinker. "We won't take up much of his time, but I'm afraid it's urgent."

"Mr. Croxton is a busy man."

"Dutch Sawyer sent us," said Tank. "It's about Danny Hogan."

Mr. Hogan, up until last week, had been the most notorious of St. Paul's underworld figures, the one responsible for the agreement between the criminals and the St. Paul police department that, as long as no crimes were committed within the city limits, criminals would not be arrested or handed over for deeds committed elsewhere.

That was until a bomb planted under his car had reduced him to a pile of ash.

Mr. Sawyer, Mr. Hogan's second-in-command, had ordered Tank and Tinker to discover who killed his boss. Struggling to hang on to Mr. Hogan's subordinates and keep all-out warfare from breaking out in the streets, he simply didn't have the time or the brainpower to devote to it.

Finding out who had killed Hogan would go a long way to calming things down.

Or so he'd claimed. It wasn't as if Tank and Tinker had a choice. They owed the mob, they had to pay up. Their flimsy list of potential leads thus far led them to the track. The Polar Star Racetrack & Casino was the newest and largest greyhound racing complex anywhere west of Boston.

It was one of the only places they had that might remotely turn into a lead.

Whether it was the power of the name 'Dutch Sawyer,' or just hearing the metal giant speak, the man before Tank and Tinker turned milky pale under his tan. "All right, all right, why didn't you say so?" he asked. He reached around and pulled a switch with a three-fingered claw-like hand that glistened dull metal; how much of the rest of his arm was also a prosthetic was concealed beneath his shirt sleeve. Tinker guessed that like most amputees his age that the man was a Great War veteran.

The gate retracted just enough to admit Tank's bulk, though he had to duck to avoid clanging his head on the rounded ceiling, which extended for about fifty feet beyond the gate. Once through the entrance tunnel the room opened up into a grand foyer.

Tinker whistled. She and Tank both stopped and took everything in. It was hard to tell if Tank was as awed as Tinker felt, since his smooth silver face couldn't change expressions, but if she had to guess she would say their feelings were probably quite similar.

The room was three stories high, and at each level balconies looked down onto the main floor. The balcony railings, made of gleaming golden metal, curved out into the main space at seemingly random intervals. The walls were white marble, inlaid with large black marble and smaller golden circles in abstract designs. Her eye caught by a reflection of glass, Tinker looked closer and saw that there were light bulbs also set into the walls. They were off at the moment, but when illuminated, she would bet they gave the illusion of shining stars.

A crystal chandelier that was probably as wide as Tank was tall hung from the center of...well, it should have been the ceiling, but instead most of the ceiling was an inverted dome skylight. The stained glass of the skylight was the only splash of color in the otherwise black, white and gold room, and it featured white and black greyhounds cavorting against a mostly azure blue background that winked with a rainbow of other colors.

A grand white staircase beckoned guests to the second floor, and at the top of the stairs Tinker saw the barred windows—all shuttered for the moment—where bets could be placed. Numbered entrances off this floor and the one above it must lead into the stadium itself, which Tinker had heard from her friend Minerva was completely enclosed so that races could take place no matter the weather. The noise must be tremendous when this place was at full capacity. A wide tunnel entrance to their left bore an electrical sign above it, unlit at the moment, that proclaimed it the entrance to the casino. There was a gate across this entrance as well, though this one was of a golden tone that matched the balcony rails.

Their guide stood off to the right with his silent, patient greyhound, waiting for them to finish feeling overawed with an unimpressed expression that said he'd seen this reaction a thousand times before. His arms were crossed. "This way."

He led them through a discreet side door that opened into a more functional space than the lavish area they had just left. It was much cooler in here than it had been in either the station or the grand entranceway, making Tinker glad she had not eschewed her coat or hat, though it was not so bitingly cold as the December day outside. Tank had to duck a little again in this plain industrial hallway and remain so—it was a good thing his limbs didn't get tired when he had to do this for extended periods.

The scent of dogs, and something earthier that smelled like straw or grass, tickled Tinker's nose. She held back a sneeze through sheer willpower.

The tunnel they were in curved gently to the left, and the smells of animals and straw grew more powerful.

"What is your dog's name?" asked Tank unexpectedly.

"The Queen of Sheba," the man answered. "But mostly we call her Queenie around here."

"Fitting. She's lovely."

"Thank you. She's the pride of the Polar Star, though she's recently retired from the racing life. They'll be breeding her come spring." The man reached down and stroked Queenie's golden head. The dog looked up and offered a tail wave, opening her long mouth in what looked for all the world like a grin.

"She's more docile than I would have expected, from a dog bred and trained to run for sport," said Tinker.

"Oh, for the most part they're all like this, when they're not on the track. Quiet as mice, and sweet as you please, even the big males. I keep Queenie with me because she enjoys the out-and-abouts. On the track, it's a different story. You'll see. We'll be passing the track in a minute, and they'll be training up some saplings."

"Saplings?" asked Tinker.

"Young'ns."

No more was said until they came around a tighter bend and indeed, had a view of the track from the ground level through a series of large windows of slightly rippled glass. Their guide paused, and so did they, to watch as with a clash of gears the starter box opened and five lanky greyhounds spilled out. Four of them immediately charged after the lure, a fur-covered form about rabbit sized that ran along a single track not dissimilar to the one the high-speed trolleys ran on, albeit on a smaller scale. The fifth greyhound, striped in black and reddish brown like a tiger, trotted off to sniff and wave his tail at the dirt, seemingly unconcerned that his fellows were competing to try to catch the lure, which stayed just enough ahead to avoid being caught even by the swiftest of them.

Around the track oval they went, legs pumping, spines going up and down rhythmically with their powerful strides. The fifth greyhound had to scrabble to get out of the way when they came back around the track and started on a second loop, but still he did not appear inclined to join in.

Their guide snorted. "That one's a dud for sure. Never seen a grey in all my born days less interested in the chase. He's no good for racing."

"What will happen to him?"

A shrug and bland face were the response.

Tinker narrowed her eyes and bit the inside of her cheek, but said nothing. It wasn't really any of her business.

She heard gears whirr and the slight scrape of Tank's metal overlays moving against each other as he shifted from foot to foot, a very human gesture reflecting discomfort. She knew that it couldn't be that his physical form was tired, so it must be that he'd picked up on the man's deliberate ambiguity as well. But he didn't press the issue.

They watched until the racers crossed the finish line, past a human timekeeper with his stopwatch. The times were recorded in a book held by yet another man, and a few boys who looked about fifteen or sixteen rounded up the dogs. Once the mechanical lure had disappeared through a special gateway, the pack had slowed down and were now gamboling with their compatriot who had refused to race, all sniffing and yipping and chasing each other and waving their whip-like tails in great excitement. While clearly winded,

none of them seemed overextended and
bounced about as they were each caught in
turn and a lead cord slipped around their
necks. The boys catching them offered pats
and ruffled ears. One dog, the biggest,
jumped up to put his paws on his boy's
shoulders and gave him a long-tongued kiss
right across the face. The boy forced him
back down, laughing. The striped rebel
greyhound was giving his boy some trouble,
letting him get almost close enough and
then bounding away. Tinker stifled a
giggle, watching.

"Come on, then, if you've looked your
fill." Their guide led them on past rows
of straw-bedded kennels, some of which
were filled with resting or alert
greyhounds. They didn't seem particularly
distressed at their confinement, and most
of them raised their heads or offered tail
waves. Their guide was right that they
made very little noise. Tinker had been
expecting a great deal more barking with
so many dogs in such close quarters. A few
got up to brush noses with Queenie as she

went by, but they didn't appear distressed that they couldn't join her in wandering the facility.

All of the dogs ignored Tinker and Tank equally beyond idle curiosity towards a stranger in their home. Animals were rarely troubled by the strangeness that was Tank the way people were; in fact, he was a favorite napping perch to Tinker's pack of workshop cats thanks to the slight warmth his circuits gave off.

Once past the kennels, they entered a row of identical nondescript whitewashed doors. A few were open, revealing small offices with desks. At the far end was a polished wooden door of a far better quality than the others. Their guide went up to it and knocked.

"Mr. Croxton, there's a...a...some guests, to see you. They say they're sent by Dutch Sawyer."

"Let 'em in," said a deep voice from behind the door, with a distinctive Boston dockside brogue.

Their guide opened the door and gestured for Tank and Tinker to enter. Tinker went first, if only to get a look at Mr. Croxton's expression while he watched Tank squeeze through the door. She never got tired of seeing how disconcerted people got upon first beholding the marvel that was Tank. Reading about him in the papers never did justice to the sheer size of him, or how despite his size all of his joints fitted together neatly without angry squeals of metal.

Mr. Croxton himself was a man in his mid-fifties, squat with thinning hair that must normally be covered by the brown bowler hat that sat on his desk. He wore a brown wool suit that looked new, and a red tie.

In one corner of the office, sitting up to examine the intruders, lay yet another greyhound on a neatly folded bed of sheepskin. This one was coal black, with white paws, a white stripe on its chest, and an unusual arched nose that made it look as if it might have been crossed with something other than a greyhound. It rumbled deep in its chest.

"Easy, Dodge," Mr. Croxton said, waving a hand at it. The dog, apparently Dodge, subsided, though he still watched them with great intensity out of eyes so light a brown they were almost gold.

"So." Mr. Croxton leaned back in his chair—he hadn't bothered to rise when they entered, and certainly made no attempt to shake hands. "What does Dutch want, that he sent the Tin Man and his little Dorothy to lean on me? I bet it's to do with ol' Danny's death."

"Yes, it does," Tinker said, holding on to her temper at his dismissive tone and rude nicknames. "We're looking into Mr. Hogan's outstanding business affairs. He loaned you quite a bit of money to build this place, according to his books."

"And I made the agreed-upon payments like clockwork, which should also be in those books," said Mr. Croxton. "I can show youze ours, if you like."

"That would be very helpful, thank you," replied Tinker. "Now, if you don't mind. Then we'll be on our way."

"Of course. Don't take too long. It's a big place I got to run, in case youze haven't noticed." Mr. Croxton pulled a heavy, black leather-bound book embossed with the Polar Star Racetrack & Casino constellation logo in silver and thrust it at them across the desk. Tinker started to reach forward, but Tank was faster and caught it before it hit the floor. His metal head stayed focused on Mr. Croxton, who turned visibly paler but valiantly maintained his neutral expression.

Tank passed Tinker the book and she immediately appreciated that he had grabbed it first. It was heavy, and she probably would have been unable to catch it without staggering and losing her dignity. An important thing to maintain, if they were to keep the upper hand in this encounter. She shot Tank a subtle, grateful look, and flipped open the book.

She kept her own books for her repair business, so she knew perfectly well how to skim a ledger. Everything from the past year seemed on the up-and-up; the payment records matched not only regular payments and interest on the loan to construct the Polar Star that they had seen in Mr. Hogan's books, but also Mr. Hogan's cut of the gambling profits from both the races and the casino. Tinker suppressed the urge to whistle as she did some quick mental mathematics. The amount of money coming through this place in a single weekend of racing was more than her entire family, including her parents and older brother, could earn in their lifetimes. If this was correct, Mr. Croxton could well afford to pay back the loan, even with the ridiculously high interest rate Hogan had been charging him.

She placed the book back on the desk and slid it across.

"So, you see, I had no reason to want Danny dead," said Mr. Croxton. "He'n I understood each other. Terrible, what happened to him, but youze can tell Dutch I had nothin' to do with it and he can poke his suspicious nose elsewhere. I'd say sumthin' less polite, but my Ma taught me to respect a lady." The look he gave Tinker told her he thought her anything but ladylike, but he didn't dare say anything outright disparaging in case her still-silent metal shadow took exception to his language.

"I'll tell Mr. Sawyer you were nothing but helpful," Tinker replied sweetly, acid in her eyes. "Thank you for taking the time to see us."

Tank opened the door and let her go through first, then squeezed himself out. Once he'd shut the door behind himself and they were some distance down the hall, Tinker grumbled, "Well, that was a dead end."

"We still have more places to look," Tank pointed out.

"This one just seemed the most likely given how much money he owed, though I had no idea just how much money this place makes."

"I can understand the excitement," Tank said. "And racing the dogs takes out the human element of horse racing. I see the appeal, especially after so many horses were lost in the Great War."

"At least he appears to treat his dogs well," Tinker said. They had reached the hallway with the kennels, and she gestured around. The greyhounds surrounding them were lean, muscular creatures with beautiful glossy coats. Their individual kennels were neat and clean. A few of them had minor injuries, but they had been tended with liniment and bandages.

"It wouldn't be profitable to have sick or starving animals. Not if they want them performing at their best for the crowds," said Tank, as dismissive as she had ever heard from him.

"Oh, I'm not fooled into thinking Mr. Croxton is anything but a businessman. But he's got people working for him who give a damn about this place, to have everything about it so neat and tidy and the dogs so content. It's almost annoying, how perfect it all is. I so wanted it to be him. Then our job would have been easy, and we'd have Dutch Sawyer off our backs."

Tank's only reply was a pleasant tonal hum that might have been agreement, or might have been only trying to sound agreeable.

"Is your sound processor malfunctioning again?" Tinker asked, grinning to let him know she was teasing.

Tank upped the volume on the tone.

"What was that, I didn't hear you?" Tinker said, cupping a hand to her ear.

Tank upped the volume a little more, and they both laughed, a rare sound from the usually serious, quiet Tank.

Tinker didn't know whether he'd been like that in his previous life or if his time trapped in the old war tank unable to speak beyond grinding gears had conditioned him to listen first and talk second, but she cherished the times she managed to get him to display his buried sense of humor.

They both sobered as the sound of paws approached them from further up the corridor. But instead of their guide coming to fetch them and lead them out, as they had expected, a greyhound trotted alone around the gentle curve. And it wasn't golden Queenie, but the striped dog who had had so little interest in racing. At least, Tinker was fairly certain they were one and the same. Up close, she saw this dog had a slightly crooked tail, as if it had been broken once about midway down, that she vaguely remembered seeing on the playful dog from the track.

"Hey," said Tinker in the gentle voice usually reserved for her cats, "what are you doing out?"

The dog stopped a few feet away and just stood there, waving its tail idiotically. Then it pivoted on its long, powerful hindquarters and trotted back the way it came. Tank and Tinker looked at each other, and in unspoken agreement

followed along behind. Tinker half-hoped
she could catch it by the strip of leather
around its neck and perhaps return it to
human hands before they left to pursue
their next lead. For whatever good that
would do.

Tinker kept expecting to see their
human guide, or someone else, pop out and
ask them what they were doing. But though
they saw glimpses through windows of men
working on the track itself preparing
another practice race, they were focused
on getting the fractious young saplings in
the starting gate and did not notice
either the loose greyhound, Tinker, or
even Tank's large bulk making their way
through the underbelly of the stadium.

The greyhound paused at a door and
scratched at it. Then he turned a looked
pitifully up at Tinker—from behind Tinker
could definitely tell that it was a 'he.'
She turned the knob and opened the door,
ready to apologize to whoever was behind
it. The dog slipped inside, and Tinker
could see that this was an office recently

in use. Although it was deserted at the moment, there was an electric furnace in one corner. The warmth emanating from it prickled Tinker's skin and drew her to step partway through the door. No wonder the dog had wanted to go in. Indeed, it had immediately settled next to the furnace and gave a long sigh. Clever thing. It must have slipped out of its crate somehow.

Tinker shook her head and was about to move on and close the door when she noticed a ledger similar to the one Mr. Croxton had shown them sitting on the edge of the desk.

She glanced around to make sure no one else was in view.

Tank tilted his round domed head quizzically when she locked eyes with him but said nothing.

She shrugged, slipped into the room and opened the book. Out of the corner of her eye she saw Tank take up a post beside the door, presumably so that he could warn her if anyone came. Though what they would do at that point was anyone's guess, since Tinker would be caught with her hand in the proverbial cookie jar and no one here would take kindly to that. Tank did have energy weapons built into secret compartments in both forearms and another, larger one in his back, that Tinker had designed in deference to his previous shell as a true tank (these were high among the reasons Mr. Sawyer had wanted involved in investigating Mr. Hogan's death to begin with). But neither Tank nor Tinker wanted to resort to shooting their way out if they could avoid it.

Tinker skimmed the pages and quickly discovered that she was indeed looking at a duplicate of the book she had just read in Mr. Croxton's office. However, there were a few key differences, of which she discovered the origins when she flipped to the latest entries. The loan from Danny Hogan, and its payments, did not appear, nor were they referenced. Instead, a different loan, from someone named Frank

Wallace in Boston, showed, also with installed payments.

Tinker marked her spot with a finger and flipped back, her brain running furious calculations. Everything else in the two books appeared the same, and if that were true—

"Something is definitely rotten here," she murmured. "Tank, this might be—"

Tank let out a soft, strumming tone that sounded vaguely as if someone had brushed their fingers against harp strings—a sound that would alert her but not someone listening for a human voice. Tinker shut the book, and, after a moment's hesitation, hefted it and tucked it under an arm to carry with her. Maybe showing it to Mr. Sawyer would be proof enough that Mr. Croxton hadn't been completely honest, and he could take it up with Mr. Wallace of Boston, whoever he was. Tank and Tinker would be out of it. Perhaps by discovering this, their debt would be paid.

She could dream, anyway. It was worth the risk.

When she moved to the door, to her surprise the greyhound stood and came with her. They slipped back out into the hallway and Tinker closed the door behind them. She motioned with her head that they should start walking towards the exit, and Tank nodded vigorously.

Tinker soon found herself slightly left behind since both of her companions could walk much more quickly than she could, especially since she was stuck in a skirt and heeled shoes. She cursed her choice to be respectable for this venture and wished she'd worn boy's clothes and her work boots and her feminine reputation be damned. Boy's clothes were easier to escape potentially hostile situations in.

"Hey! Stop!" came a shout from behind.

Tinker cursed under her breath and tried to lengthen her stride, but only succeeded in almost turning her ankle. She cursed again, louder.

Tank skidded to a halt and came back for her. He reached her side just as their guide came around the corner, red in the face and huffing. The man looked angry; both his fists were clenched and his jaw was set.

"Just what do you think—" he started, and then abruptly closed his mouth when Tank pushed Tinker behind him and extended his right arm, popping out the concealed energy weapon.

The man's face went from red to white in the space of a few seconds, and he raised both hands—the living one and the scratched metal claw-prosthetic—in a gesture of surrender. Even if he'd never seen an energy weapon before, it looked enough like a traditional explosion-propulsion gun that its purpose was obvious. As was the threat. "Easy," he said. "Don't shoot." His eyes darted to the book in Tinker's hand and widened.

"Let us go, and don't tell anyone what you saw," said Tank in a voice just loud enough to be heard. "It's the easiest way

for you to stay clear of anything between
Mr. Sawyer and Mr. Croxton. We'd like to
avoid collateral damage."

"You got it," their guide replied, eyes
still on the energy weapon. "They don't
pay me enough for this," he muttered under
his breath.

"We don't even know your name," Tinker
said. "That way, if anyone asks, we can
truthfully say we don't know anyone at the
Polar Star besides Mr. Croxton. I'm
sorry," she felt compelled to add, "we
didn't want this, either."

"I let you go, nobody says anything,
then we're even," he said. He backed away,
hands still in the air.

"What about the dog?" Tank asked.

Tinker glanced around to find that the
striped greyhound was peering around from
behind her, ears pricked, posture watchful
and hopeful all at once.

"Keep him, if he'll go with you," the
man said. "He has less than a future
here."

Tinker opened her mouth to protest, but Tank turned his head to shoot her a look with his cool, unblinking lightbulb eyes and she swallowed it. What to do with the dog once it was out of the Polar Star complex was a problem they could sort out later. Right now, they needed to escape while there was only one witness.

She swore under her breath again. "Come on," she said, louder, turning to find the door to the grand entryway about twenty feet down the corridor. Tank retracted his weapon and began to back towards the door. Tinker and the dog stepped sideways to get out of his way and they all went through the door.

Back out into the grand entryway, the tunnel, and to the trolley station they hightailed it as fast as they could walk and still appear casual. The book remained tucked securely under Tinker's arm, though she could feel sweat from her hand starting to make it difficult to grip. She hit the button to let the next trolley know to stop for them with a bit too much force. The slamming sound echoed all around the still-deserted station.

Fortunately non-hooved animals were permitted on the trolleys, so not one of the few passengers raised an eyebrow when they entered with a greyhound in tow. Getting the greyhound up the steps to the trolley was an interesting endeavor that involved Tinker encouraging from the top while Tank gently lifted the hindquarters, and in the end the dog made the leap in one single, surprising bound that had Tinker staggering back.

"We'll have to work on that, if we ever do this again," Tinker said, wiping the sweat from her brow and taking a firm grip on the dog's leather collar with one hand. Then with the other she readjusted her hold on the book, and finally dropped into a seat with a huge sigh. Tank sat next to her with more care.

Once they pulled away from the station, some of Tinker's tension eased. She was also preoccupied soothing the greyhound, which was quivering and looking all around for the source of the noise that the trolley made as it moved along its track. He calmed considerably when Tank reached out and placed a large metal hand on its shoulders.

"What are you doing?" Tinker whispered out of the side of her mouth.

"I am vibrating internally at a specific frequency I have found the cats appreciate," said Tank.

"Oh."

Tank was finding new uses for the body she had created for him all the time, making it more and more his own. Tinker had found this to also be true for those for whom she had designed prosthetic limbs in the past who came back to her for repairs, but it was a little astonishing to be witnessing the process up close, and at as large a scale as an entire body. She'd always known they were in uncharted territory, off the end of the map in the prosthetics field and into something else entirely, but it was in moments like this that it was driven home anew.

And in the meantime, they had a sapling greyhound to find a home for. Though Tinker had a sneaking suspicion, watching Tank pet the leggy creature and it offer him that big grin that looked so undignified on such an elegant creature, that her workshop cats might have to make room for a new resident.

At least for now.

Tinker clutched the book tighter. It might be the key to getting them all out from under the thumb of the mob for good.

"We don't even know his name," she realized.

"I'm sure we'll think of something."

Uh oh, thought Tinker. Yes, there was definitely some work ahead if she ever intended to pry the greyhound away from their little family. Not that her heart was one hundred percent into any thoughts of prying. The greyhound's big, innocent brown eyes were all too quickly worming their way into her affections.

She reached out and scratched him underneath his pointed chin. He flicked his ears forward, and his expression made her melt a little inside. He would be a huge hit with Minerva, who had gushed about the greyhounds' beauty for days after each of her visits to the Polar Star.

But those were all secondary to getting out of the mob's grasp before she and Tank became more than just errand runners. Then she could worry about whether or not the greyhound could stay, and she knew Tank still wanted to find out as much about his own origins as they could manage—the little they knew was tantalizing, and nothing more.

For now, she could take comfort in this small victory of saving one life from what would likely have been an unpleasant fate.

She hoped it might be an omen of things to come.

We Might be Villains

By Tara Moeller

Ignore the old woman that needs some help.

Turn an eye away from the plastic bottle that falls from the bag, and rolls to the curb to crush against the concrete.

Kick away the cigarette butts that gather in the corner, the ashes that float to the ground, the smoke that litters the air we try to breathe.

We might be villains, standing by, paralyzed by indecision, by a lack of time, a scourge of give a damn, the hole in our hearts that lets the world drift through, tainted and unchanged.

Pretend it didn't happen: the gunfight last night across town, the kid one street over that disappeared, the other that cried hungry and hurt every night before bed.

We might be villains, covering our ears, closing our mouths, stifling the protests, ours and everyone else's.

Don't worry that energy is leaking away, used for unending texts and tweets and uploads and downloads.

Don't fret that the earth is running out, and no spare battery pack awaits for the recharge.

Don't be anxious; there's enough for you to waste.

We might be villains, using up, leaving out, dumping everywhere.

We might be villains, but we don't care.

Steamed Pudding

By E. G. Gaddess

The chugging clank of the outer door woke Julio from his slumber. He blinked, swiped his eyes with his right hand, rubbing the thumb and pointer finger into the corners to dig out the sleepy seeds. He yawned and stretched, scratching at things best left unscratched, and looked around the warm kitchen.

The flames for the steam oven licked around the metal boiler, the bellows pumping steam into the reservoir around its stone innards. The fire beneath the cooking pot snapped at the charred logs. Beneath the logs, the undulating orange red glow of the coals indicated the fire had been going for a long time.

He took a deep breath and the moist aroma of Haggy's cooking filling his lungs: vanilla and cinnamon, and maybe, just maybe, a hint of cardamom.

Cardamom. An expensive spice, kept locked away in a metal bin in the dark depths of the pantry. Cardamom meant someone special was coming to see the Master.

Julio groaned. *Special* meant the Master would be out to impress, to make a distinction, to come more than just the Master of the keep. *Special* meant extra work.

"Ah, you're awake at last. I wondered if I was going to have to rouse you with a cold splashing." Haggy, ancient with white wisps she called hair and few teeth, stooped over the sink. Her wet, soapy hands rested on the edge, dripping back into the reservoir.

Julio shivered and rubbed his arms. Haggy didn't waste; the splashing would be with old wash water, foul and dank and sour smelling - it was enough to make the troll sniff and lick at him. And he'd need a bath.

"Well, take your piss in the chamber pot quick-like. We got lots of work today. The King's come to visit."

The King? Why was the King coming here?

Julio forgot what he was doing, let go of himself and missed the chamber pot.

The King didn't like anyone odd, whether born or made. Haggy had told him so. The old cook had also told him about the King's parents, and how they had encouraged the creation of odds, been patrons of many of the scientists that performed the experiments.

Julio's parents had been made odd by experiments, just like Haggy, or so the old woman had told him. They had been executed for having a child together that was born odd. Julio didn't know how Haggy knew, or how he'd escaped the raid on their home, only that he'd woken up, bruised and scratched, in his corner of the kitchen, and Haggy'd kept him hidden ever since.

He got a rag and cleaned up his mess, scrubbing at the wall where the golden droplets glistened in the firelight. He hoped Haggy hadn't seen, but figured he'd better do a good job, just in case.

The outer door stopped its dirge and Julio unlocked the inner door. It creaked and groaned, and wood rasped against stone, the thick heavy door creeping up from the counterweight. Between the doors - outer closed and inner open - was a wooden bin on wheels. Julio picked up the leather belt, slinging it over his shoulder and pulled, pushing his feet against the floor, leaning into the belt. The bin jerked into the room, stopping when the rusted wheels hit wooden chocks set in the floor; the chain, run through a slit in the outer door and attached to the other end, was taut and humming.

Julio stood and moved to the back of the bin.

"Oy, loosen up." Haggy's voice echoed in the plenum chamber, making the rats that lived in it scurry away, their magnified scuffles rough and echoing and huge. The chain went lax and Julio unclipped it from the back of the bin, darting his fingers away just before the chain whipped back through the hole, spinning and clinking its dance back to the outside.

Laughter drifted down from outside, the cackle tripping up Julio's spine, tip-toeing on his skin so that goose bumps erupted.

"Did we catch you, four eyes?" The voice amplified and followed by cackling laughter.

Haggy huffed and kept to her work.

Julio scowled and peeked into the bin: Potatoes. The tubers smelled of the earth and still bore bits of fragrant peat on their skins. He'd have to wash them good before peeling them.

The inner door lowered, moving faster than when it went up. Julio stood back from it, careful to keep anything from slipping beneath the stone. He kept watch on the other side of the door, too. Though he didn't like the rats, if one got caught beneath the door, it was a bloody mess to clean up. He didn't have time for that today.

The door chinked into place, settling into the groove that sealed the kitchens from the outside. Julio wasn't sure if it sealed to keep folks out, or to keep folks in. He pushed the lever down that locked the door. Haggy made sure Julio knew to lower it after the door shut.

Hands on hips, Julio glanced to the large water clock on top of the cabinet. It was only mid-morning; there was lots of time to get the potatoes done for an evening feast.

Julio sucked on his cheek, glancing to Haggy at the sink. He wanted to see the King, see the bright banners and soldiers marching in uniform. He'd never seen the King before; hadn't seen any person but Haggy that he could remember. If he was quick...

He darted to the tall ladder that led to the single dirty window set high in the wall. Dingy sun crept through, painting a faint rectangle of yellow on the far wall.

"Git down from there!" Haggy grabbed his arm, jerking him down from the third rung. "You know ye cain't let anyone see you. Specially not today."

She shook at his arm and his head wobbled, his teeth clacking together, biting on his tongue so that fresh blood sparked his mouth with tinny taste. He tried to nod, but didn't think she could tell; she was shaking him too hard. "Yessum, Haggy."

The old cook stared at him, bottom lip jutted out. Her eyes narrowed and she looked him up and down before nodding once.

"Hmmph. Time to git to work." She let go his arm and scuffled to the ovens.

Julio glanced to the big copper cooking pot, its bottom blackened by the soot of decades of fires. It took up the whole center of the room, sitting at the end of a wide trench of ashes and embers, a slight ring of stones encircled the thick logs used for fuel. A winch and chains rose above it; a cracked wooden lever let

the cook lift and move it around the
kitchen.

Haggy usually had the troll do that for
her. The troll didn't mind. Haggy fed it
and tended its wounds. And it was strong,
far stronger than Julio and Haggy
together.

Julio had been afraid of the troll when
he'd first arrived, only his clothes and
blanket familiar. But now, he considered
it a pet, similar to a dog or cat like the
uppers had. Only better; a troll was far
more useful.

He thought about that first meeting -
the stinky troll drooling in the corner,
orange tongue licking its snot. Julio
thought he might have missed his parents,
but he couldn't remember. His parents were
shadows in his mind, lurking at the
fringes of memory, making him
uncomfortable but not sad. A drifting
memory of lemon and sage, of a mesmerizing
lilt of song, enough to make one forget to
breathe. He also remembered fire and fear

and gentle hands holding him out a window into strange, strangling arms.

He wondered about them sometimes, but he had Haggy and the troll, and while he wished he could play in the sun, he was content to live safe in the kitchen.

Julio picked up his stool and set it next to the large pot, but far enough from the fire he wouldn't get burned. He stepped up and stared into it, on tip toe to keep his nose clear of the metal pot. The fire crackled, lapping its hot yellow tongues over thick oak logs. Heat rose, steam drifted up, bubbles burst from the surface.

"Ouch!" Julio drew back, one hand to his cheek where thick yellow custard had flown upward and landed. It burned, thick and hot, and he knew his skin would be pink and puffed. But... he smelled sugar and vanilla. He took the bit from his cheek and touched it to his tongue. The sugar and spice rushed at his tongue, making his mouth water, and he sighed. He pulled the scents into the deepest recesses of his lungs. Maybe they would catch there, and later, he could pull them out and smell them again. Maybe he could do that at night, when the ovens were cold and he shivered under his thin blanket.

"Get away from that pot." Haggy used a large wooden spoon to swat Julio's bottom.

Julio jumped from the stool, one hand rubbing the sore cheek on his face, the other the sore cheek on his behind. "Wha'd ye do that for?"

"Te keep ye from fallin' in." Haggy hobbled to the pot and stirred two-handed to move the thick sauce. "I don't want it burnt and I don't want it flavored with the essence of filthy boy."

Julio wanted to stick his tongue out at Haggy, but she had eyes in the back of her head, and she'd give him a hard smack for sure.

Beneath the long white tendrils on the back of her head, one blue eye and one green eye blinked and looked around, each in its own direction. Julio watched those eyes, for those eyes could see everything, even in the dark it seemed. Those eyes could spot trouble coming or going, or a dirty mouse in the corner needing a trap. Or a tiny boy crying silent in the corner.

Haggy'd gotten the eyes when she'd been young. She'd been turned out of her job as a maid in a fancy house when the mistress had caught the lordship looking at her too long. So, she'd volunteered for the old king's experiments – and the money they brought - and wound up with the extra eyes. When young, she'd been able to keep them covered; back then, her hair had been lustrous and thick, and only her close friends had known. She'd used those eyes to keep a look out while she took what she needed; she'd never had to worry about her lookout talking on her.

But now, furrowed and bent nearly in two, hair long gone with her distant childhood, those extra eyes were where all could see them, so she worked alone in the kitchen – except for Julio and the troll. Julio didn't much mind the extra eyes. He wasn't sure the troll knew any better.

Sometimes, he wondered what difference his parents had had. Extra eyes like Haggy? Maybe extra ears or an extra nose? Maybe...?

Julio wiped his three hands — one right and two left — on his trousers.

"Oy, keep them hands clean."

He couldn't help but roll his eyes. He trudged to the big porcelain sink, pulling the wooden step stool with him. He dragged the feet on the floor, leaving little trails in the wet left by the condensing steam.

Julio turned on the hot water spigot, testing it with his second left hand. That was the extra hand and it didn't feel as good as the other two. It wasn't as fast either, or the fingers as nimble. Sometimes, it fell asleep on him, and it was all he could do to keep from crying out from the sharp prickles when it woke up. He soaped them all and scrubbed them all and rinsed them all then held them up for Haggy to see.

"Good boy. Now get to work." Haggy turned to the ovens, opening the door to a blast of heat, the force of it making the wisps dance on her forehead. "Why h'ain't you peeling them potatoes yet?"

Picking up a potato with his first left hand and rinsing the peat off in running cold water, Julio started peeling with a knife in his right. Once done, he rinsed it again and picked up another potato with the second left hand and started peeling it before the first was tossed into the boiling pan.

Peeling and shucking and snapping was what Julio did. In the kitchen, his third hand was an advantage – same as Haggy's extra eyes. She could watch the pot on the hearth while kneading the bread dough. He didn't like it so much at night; it grew out below his regular left arm, and he usually wound up sleeping on it and it would go all numb and take forever to feel right again.

"Ye'll do your chores quick-like if'n you want some of that there pudding."

Haggy stopped stirring and tapped the spoon on the side of the pot. Thick yellow custard fell back into the pot.

Julio's stomach rumbled. Oh, he wanted some of the pudding. The crispy, cinnamon – and today, cardamom, too - flavored cake cooking in the steam oven, served coated in the sweet creamy custard was Haggy's signature dish. People from all over came to eat it – now, even the King himself wanted a taste.

Julio kept quiet, peeling and rinsing the potatoes, and the bin got emptier and the boiling pan fuller. By noon, he had to lean into the bin, fishing around the bottom to find a potato. He fell in only once, and Haggy scolded him and made him wash his hands all over again.

When he was done, he jumped down from his stool. He was too little to move the potato pot to the fire, but he could swing the water pipe and fill it, and sprinkle salt from the box that Haggy was supposed to keep locked up but never did.

"Do you think we'll get any meat tonight?" Julio imagined the fire pit outside and someone grilling a boar on a spit. Maybe two, or even three, since there were so many guests. The King warranted more than the scrawny chickens Haggy usually had to cook. Julio and Haggy usually got to eat the soup made from the bones and the old carrots that you could bend without making them snap in two.

Haggy snorted into the bread, pinching out the piece of boogered dough and throwing it to the floor. The old troll, half blind and full stupid, picked it up and ate it, smacking and curling his lips in pleasure. "The Master'll be lucky to get meat tonight. The King and his men mean to take all they can. That's what they do."

"Oh." Julio slumped his shoulders and kicked at the wet floor.

"Don't you worry, though. We'll be eating well. Just you wait."

Julio nodded and prodded the troll with a finger. The troll squinted at him,

puckering its puce-tinted lips. Julio
pointed to the potato pot then to the
hearth.

The troll knew what it was supposed to
do. It was well trained and very helpful,
if a little unthinking. It lumbered to the
pot on all fours, knuckle down, and stood
hunched to hook a winch chain to the
handle and swing it over the fire. It was
a graceful movement, troll and pot
swinging together so that the water didn't
even slosh.

Haggy smiled and pinched off more bread
dough; one piece for the troll and one for
Julio.

Julio grinned and took the soft, yeasty
treat, squeezing it between his fingers.
There was no way he'd get a piece of it
cooked but for a hard heel left by one of
the scullery maids. The dough would make
his stomach bubble and he'd be burping
tonight, but it was better than an empty
stomach.

The troll sat back in its corner,
licking its piece of dough in leisure.

Julio thought it might be looking for the salty booger from the last piece, but wouldn't say so in front of Haggy. He didn't want to forfeit his promised bit of pudding.

Haggy finished rolling and balling the dough and placed it on trays and put them in the dry oven. Julio noticed an extra small loaf set just inside the door, and thought maybe he and Haggy would have it for themselves, but pushed the thought away so as not to jinx it.

The old woman moved back to the hearth and her pot of custard. She took the big spoon and stirred, releasing even more vanilla scent.

Julio's mouth watered and he swallowed down the spit. No use wasting it by drooling.

"Fetch me one of them chipped bowls." Haggy jerked her head, jowls jiggling, toward where their personal dishes were stored.

He went to the crooked cupboard — one leg was missing and an old pot with a hole was set upside down under to prop it up in the one corner. Haggy kept the chipped dishes in there; she and Julio ate off them when there was food left over. He reached for a small one from the bottom shelf.

"Nope. Fetch one of the big ones."

Julio didn't question Haggy, but reached up two more shelves, stretching high, for the bigger bowls. There weren't many bowls on the high shelf; there wasn't much sense saving them. There were never enough leftovers for a big bowl.

Haggy took the bowl and ladled custard into it. Steam spiraled up, looking of more substance than Haggy's hair. "That ought to be enough."

She slid the bowl to the far corner of the counter and covered it with a towel. "It'll be a bit watered on top, but it can't be helped." She shook her head and checked on the potatoes. "We'll be happy no matter what we get."

Julio hid a grin and wriggled. It sounded like that big bowl of custard was for them!

Next, Haggy took the big pan of pudding from the steam oven. The pudding was raised high on the sides of the pan, brown and crisped on top, but Julio knew it would be moist and buttery on the inside. Haggy knew how to make her pudding.

Julio jumped up and down. "Did you put raisins in it?"

Haggy nodded. "Yup, you know I did."

"And bits of dried apple?"

"That, too."

Julio sighed and stopped jumping. If the King was here, they wouldn't get any of the pudding. You couldn't just cut into it and take a piece, like you could take a bit of the custard. It would leave a scoop missing and someone would ask after it.

Haggy took a small pan from the counter and set it in the oven. She unhooked the bellows and let the flames that heated the steam die.

Haggy winked at him and tended to the boiling potatoes. They were nearly done.

"Troll."

The troll looked up from his licking, shoving the bit of cough into one cheek.

Haggy crooked her finger and it popped the last bit of dough in its mouth and rose. It took the potatoes from the hearth, its big calloused hands impervious to the hotness of the handle, and took it to the sink to pour out the water.

Julio knew to stand back. The water could burn, make your skin bubble and burst, if it splashed on you.

The troll didn't seem bothered by the splashing though, and stood there until all the extra water was out of the pot.

It squatted there, in front of the pot, waiting.

"Let me check the bread."

Haggy opened the other oven, the one heated directly by the flames, and checked the bread. The warm aroma of yeast reached Julio. It smelled almost as good as the pudding.

Someone knocked at the interior door.
"Half an hour."

"Hmph." Haggy limped back to the potato pot and looked in, squinting with one eye. "Julio, fetch me the tub of butter and the jug of cream from the larder."

"Yessum." Julio trotted to the small room and pushed the wooden door in. It was a step down into the dark cold, but Julio knew the room like the back of all three of his hands. He jumped down and counted his steps across the room to the alcove cut into the stone: one, two, three, four, and a half. He picked up the pot and the jug and hugged them to his chest.

Back in the kitchen, he handed first the butter to Haggy and waited for her to dump it into the pot before handing her the jug. Then she poured in half the cream, stamping down the soft potatoes with a long-handled screen into a lumpy mash.

"Troll."

The troll stood where he squatted, holding out his hands for the handled screen. Haggy handed it to him and stood back but kept her eyes on the potatoes.

The troll continued the mashing, only faster. Haggy tapped the troll's shoulder and it stopped so she could add a little more cream. Soon, the potatoes were silky enough to pass for anyone else's custard.

Julio envied the fancy folks who sat at the tables in the great hall and ate off round wooden plates, lacquered so they wouldn't soak up juice and oil and turn rancid. They used knives and spoons, too, and drank from fancy gold goblets. Julio had gotten a good look at the Master's goblet once; the jewels looked like a rainbow of glistening water drops all the way around it. He wondered if the King would use the Master's goblet, and if he did, what goblet would the Master use? Could there be another goblet with such gems? Perhaps the King traveled with his own, even more splendid, goblet?

There was another knock on the wall. "Ten minutes."

Haggy snorted and took the screen from the troll, pushing him toward a large brass crank in the corner. The troll moved to the crank and started turning it. It turned slow and creaked long.

Julio covered his ears, glad he had the extra hand to help Haggy guide the potato pot to the window that was creeping open. Hands appeared at the bottom, then arms and elbows in beige shirtsleeves. These hands took the pot and pulled it through the window, not waiting for it to be open all the way.

"Hurry it up. You ain't kept around to take your time. Why the Master keeps you..." "

"Careful, don't touch her. She's been damned. You never know..."

Haggy opened the oven and pulled out the bread, handing it to other arms and hands through the window. Julio knew Haggy had good ears; she heard almost as good as she saw, but you'd never know it watching her now. Silent, lips pursed, she added what looked like more vanilla to the custard, stirring to make it glossy and pouring it over the pudding from the oven. Julio had never seen her add more vanilla at the end, but thought she must be trying extra hard to make it good for the King. The pudding was the last thing handed through the window, eight sets of hands carefully grasping the edges to carry it off.

Once it was all gone, Haggy nodded to the troll and it cranked in the opposite direction to close the window.

When it was shut, Haggy sighed, the sound a rush of old air from deep in her lungs. Julio stared at her face. Her mouth was set in a line, her eyes narrowed to slits in parallel. Her nostrils were sharp, like she'd smelled something rotten.

"Well, that's done I guess. Let's eat."

Julio ran to the corner to the waiting bowl of custard, thinking they would share it with spoons.

"No, no. Fetch three small bowls, ones with the least chips." Haggy stood at the steam oven, the door partly lowered and her hand inside, her elbow jabbing like she was poking at something.

He did as he was bid, fetching not only the bowls, but spoons, too.

"Set 'em on the counter."

After setting one spoon in each bowl, Julio retrieved the big bowl and a ladle. He knew she'd need them eventually.

"Good, boy." Haggy ruffled his hair and nodded at the bowls and spoons, the cooling custard and ladle. "You're learning right."

She opened the oven again, pulling the door down all the way, and pulled out the small pan she'd put in last.

It *was* pudding. Julio could see it raised and brown and his mouth watered so much he coughed on the amount of spit in his mouth.

Even the troll perked up at the sight of it, his yellow-green eyes wide, its tongue peeking through black lips.

Haggy divided the pudding into the three bowls, giving one the last extra-crispy scoop she took from the sides, then skimmed off the watery part of the custard from the bowl and poured the good part over the puddings. She handed bowls to the troll and Julio; Julio got the one with the extra bit of crisp.

Julio sat on the floor and stared at the pudding. Steam rose from the bowl, carrying all the mixing aromas with it. Julio moaned and dipped in his spoon, filling it to the brim before putting it into his mouth.

It was hot – too hot really to eat yet – but he didn't care if the roof of his mouth peeled off to the bone. It was good to eat something hot and not left over.

The troll wasn't eating. It pouted, its bottom lip curled over, its shoulders hunched.

Haggy leaned over and pulled out the spoon and the troll tipped the bowl up to his mouth, pouring everything in at once. It made a mess; custard and bits of pudding caught in the straggles of fur on its cheeks, but it licked it away, its

Long orange tongue lapping and curling and pulling it into its mouth.

Julio waited for Haggy to say something, but she didn't. She sat, rocking a little, spoon tapping her bowl, waiting for hers to cool.

The troll set its bowl down and retreated to its corner, curling so that it looked like a roughly woven hair rug. Only the rise and fall of its chest testified to it being a living, breathing thing.

Julio took another spoonful of pudding. It was cooler now and he could taste the vanilla and all that sweetness melting over his tongue.

"You make the best pudding, Haggy. You really do."

"Thank you, Julio. I like to think so." Haggy took her first bite of pudding, licking the custard off the spoon. "This batch was extra special."

"'cause we got our own not-leftovers?"

Haggy laughed. "Yup. 'cause we didn't have to wait for leftovers." Haggy closed her eyes and rested her head back, canted to the side so as not to bother the eyes in back. She'd only eaten half her pudding.

"Haggy? Are you okay?" Julio didn't want Haggy to be sick. He knew she was old; she'd told him she'd worked for the Master's father, had begged him for a job in the kitchen when her hair first turned white and her extra eyes out where all could see.

Haggy blinked, her front eyes watery, drops pooling to seep out the corners. "It's been a long day, Julio. Just remember, we got firsts this time. So we don't eat any leftovers. Got that? And keep the troll from eating any leftovers, too."

Julio nodded, his mouth full of custard and pudding. He'd never seen Haggy look so serious.

"Swear to me, Julio." Haggy snatched his arm, making him look at her.

"I swear, Haggy."

She smiled and let go, nodding and handing him her own bowl. "I guess I'm too tired to eat. You finish mine up. Don't forget what I said. And don't be scared if you hear strange things tonight. No one can get into the kitchen unless we let them."

Julio frowned. "But, Haggy…"

Haggy's head tilted to the side and a soft snore erupted from her.

He shrugged, finished his own pudding and hers. He put all three bowls and spoons in the sink, washing them with hot water and soap, and setting them to air dry. Then he lay down with his head on Haggy's lap, all three hands folded beneath his cheek.

# # #

A loud groaning woke Julio the next morning. He stood and stretched, scratched at what had no business being scratched, and looked for Haggy.

Haggy slouched at the oven, poking at something with a spoon, the fire below flittering, lighting up her smile.

Julio tip-toed toward the window. Weak morning light streamed through a clean spot where someone had taken a rag to it.

"Git up and take a look." Haggy scuttled to the sink, dirty spoon in hand. She waved her hands in an upward motion. "Gowan. Git up there."

Julio stared. Haggy wanted him up at the window?

"Ye don't have to worry if they sees you today." Haggy laughed, the cackles tickling Julio so that he laughed with her.

Haggy turned back to the room, but the blue eye stared at him, unblinking

"What's that noise?"

"The King and his men."

Julio shimmied up the ladder, holding tight, pulling with all his hands. At the top, he balanced on the rung, leaning his hands on the sill.

"The King? Making that awful sound?" Julio thought it sounded like the troll when it got something caught in the mouse trap trying to sneak the bit of cheese bait. He pressed his nose to the cleared bit of window, squinting when sunlight stabbed his eyes.

Soldiers in bright red jackets rolled in the grass, hands to their stomachs, vomit spewing from their mouths. Some rolled into the vomit of others, not seeming to care. They screamed and groaned and screamed again.

Someone wailed, long and wavering, from within the keep.

"And perhaps the Master, if they left him any of my pudding."

Julio stared down at Haggy; her face looked younger with sunshine lighting on it. "What was wrong with your pudding?" He put his extra left hand on his stomach, pushing to test it for pain.

"Nothing with what we ate. The pudding we ate was just like I always make"

Julio let his breath out, sagging like a wet piss rag. He crawled down the ladder, careful not to miss a step.

Haggy leaned forward when he was level with her and whispered in his ear. "But

the big one: well, that one was just a
little different."

the big one: well, that one was just a

Our Contributors:

Don't forget to check out all the
authors, poets, and artists who
contributed to this special anthology.

Travis I Sivart

Travis I. Sivart writes Speculative Fiction, Steampunk, Social DIY, SciFi, High Fantasy, and more. Travis's writing style has been described as true storytelling with the feel of sitting next to a fireplace and listening to a tale. He can be found at Amazon and other fine book retailers, as well as at TravisISivart.com. He also hosts a weekly streaming internet talk show on Twitch.tv/TalkOfTheTavern, details can be found at http://www.TalkOfTheTavern.com.

Twitch.tv/TalkOfTheTavern

Andrew Hiller

Blaved: Only the Good Parts was written in loving homage to William Goldman whose screenplays and books have provided readers and viewers with endless joy. Goldman passed on November 16, 2018.

Andrew Hiller's commentaries have been selected four times as the best of the year by DC NPR station WAMU 88.5 FM. He is also the author of two fantasy novels: *A Climbing Stock* and *A Halo of Mushrooms*.

Emberly Summers

Emberly Summers has been writing for the last 15 years. What inspires her most are nature, the fantasy and paranormal realms, musicals such as *The Phantom of The Opera* and *Wicked,* and of course, her favorite music ranging from showtunes to punk rock. She is the founder of Our Fantasy Realm, a site that covers reviews of video games and films, mythology, and poems written by fantasy writers. She is also a writer and reviewer for Gothic Bite Magazine, an e-magazine that reviews gothic films, television, and video games, as well as mythology and haunted places.

Social Media Links:
www.ourfantasyrealm.com
www.gothicbitemagazine.com

Rogues and Rebels

Jeffrey S. McGuire

Jeffrey S. McGuire is one superhero identity of Ora McGuire (Nickie Jamison). She is a writer of lgbtq+ erotica and romance blended with sci-fi, fantasy, and horror. Ora's hobbies include gaming, fan-girling, and doing marathons...on Netflix. She also vlogs about life, makeup, and KonMari decluttering on her YouTube channel. Ora lives in Hampton Roads with her darling husband and two spoiled furbabies; #thecatwecalljayne and #KAYLEEsmallFRYE. You can find her living #prettygeeky on all the social media @oopswrongcookie.

Luna Nyx Frost

Luna Nyx Frost has been writing for the last 20 years. Her inspiration mostly comes from nature, ancient history, and classic literature. But she has also looked up to the great work of poets such as Edgar Allen Poe and Emily Dickens. Because her passion for writing and reading doesn't stop at sonnets and novels, she has also read Shakespeare and fables by The Brothers Grimm. Then she wondered where it all began and so the mythologies of the great ancient civilizations awakened her imagination and she had to write stories. Her knowledge of history, fantasy, and Gothic brought her to where she is today: a writer and researcher for Gothic Bite and Our Fantasy Realm.

Social Media Links:
www.ourfantasyrealm.com
www.gothicbitemagazine.com

Tempie W. Wade

Tempie W. Wade is the award-winning author of The Timely Revolution Book Series. She is a lifelong resident of Virginia but currently resides in Williamsburg and has a great love of history and travel. The author's writing style incorporates fantasy with historically accurate events.

Find out more about her, and her books, at www.tempiewade.com.

Allison Norfolk

Allison Norfolk is the author the Hedgewitches Tales series, historical fantasy fairy tale retellings set in the first few decades of the twentieth century. She likes to pitch it as "Downton Abbey with magic." The first three books, starting with *Poppies & Roses* (a retelling of Beauty and the Beast) are available in

ebook and physical format on Amazon. They can each be read as a standalone, though they are set in a shared universe.

She is working on a full novel starring Tank and Tinker in their decopunk Twin Cities. If that's something you'd like to see, drop her a line on her author Facebook page (https://www.facebook.com/poppiesandrosesan/) and let her know!

Tara Moeller

Tara Moeller is an author and editor, and a founding member of DreamPunk Press. She's had short stories published in several anthologies and poetry in journals during her university days.

Selenophile, a full-length novel, was published by DreamPunk Press in Summer 2018.

She is slowly constructing the follow-up novel in between editing jobs, and occasionally a poem flows from her pencil.

She writes under her own name and pseudonyms, in several genres.

You can follow her on
- Twitter (@taramoeller69)
- Instagram (@tara_moeller_69)
- Facebook (www.facebook.com/Tara-Moeller-1404909723123482/)

E. G. Gaddess

E. G. Gaddess lives in Norfolk, Virginia with her husband and two cats. Her first novel, for young adults, was *Dhampyr Heritage*, published by DreamPunk Press in April 2012; it was the publishing cooperative's debut publication. The final novel in that trilogy was published in 2018.

Her latest novels are set in an alternate, steampunk universe centered on a close-knit clan in Scotia. *Ana-Stacia's Future is Up in the Air*, *Cinead Figures it Out*, and *Coleen Just Can't Picture It* are aimed at a younger YA audience and feature a cast of LGBTQIA+ characters; the series started with the e-book novella, *Riley for Real*, which features a trans character finding their true self.

You can follow her on Facebook at www.facebook.com/eggaddess and on Instagram @eggaddess.

Rogues and Rebels

John Millington and Conquest Comics

Conquest Comics was created by John Millington to assist in the development of hopeful writers, artists, and creators who desire a career in the comic book industry. Under the mentorship and guidance from John, Casey, Dan, and Amanda, with the support of the conquest team, comic books are being created, scripted, penciled, inked, colored, and lettered...when complete, these creator-owned, new and original comic creations will be published under Conquest Comics Publishing.

Over fifty individuals are involved in Conquest Comics Publishing with more talented creators appearing every day. Ranging from teenagers who are attending high school, to adults from all age ranges, finding out it is never too late to fulfill their dreams...making it into the comic book majors...

IF YOU ARE INTERESTED IN JOINING THE
CONQUEST COMICS TEAM, PLEASE CONTACT US
AT:
https://www.facebook.com/conquestpublishing/
(804) 824-9790
4852 GEORGE WASHINGTON MEMORIAL HIGHWAY
HAYES, VIRGINIA 23072

Rogues and Rebels

Portfoli-Mo

Portfoli-Mo, our favorite narwhal, is a young artist who does the final cover formatting for DreamPunk Press (as well as a lot of their own art).

Check out their work at https://portfolimo.myportfolio.com

And follow them on Instagram: @portfoli-Mo

And Facebook: www.facebook.com/portfoli.mo

Oh, and they are also an author in their own right, with their middle grade novel *Sometimes Kat, Sometimes Kev*, as well as their young adult novels *Kiss Me in Hell* and Spork. Their latest novel is the new adult, steampunk adventure *Heart of Brass* as Morven Moeller. These novels are available from www.dreampunkpress.com.